THE GHOST OF GERSTENHABERS

The
GHOST
of
GERSTENHABERS

and other Stories

GLENN LASZLO WEISS

Epigraph Books
Rhinebeck, New York

Paperback ISBN 978-1-960090-33-1

Library of Congress Control Number 2023916551

Book design by Colin Rolfe

Epigraph Books
22 East Market Street, Suite 304
Rhinebeck, New York 12572
(845) 876-4861
epigraphps.com

For Duci, Sue, Ron C., Andy M., Mik and Janet O.

CONTENTS

THE GHOST OF GERSTENHABERS

Chapter One
TIME CHANGE

It was November. Snow was in the air but it wasn't cold enough. Werner left the Bulova Building in Woodside, Queens after another backbreaking twelve-hour shift. He had worked two weeks straight attaching the little hands and second hands on the watches. Detailed work at its most precise. And then onto the railroad platform on the Long Island Railroad to wait for the eight thirty-seven to Babylon. Maybe in a year or two, he could slow down. Ida gave him such grief for working so much, so hard. Like he had a choice. He had been informed this week that these long days would be the norm for the foreseeable future. In the Pittsburgh hills, this kind of work would have been a godsend. Ida just didn't know. She didn't know that this was the way to support the family these days. A train zoomed by skipping Woodside, the tracks screaming. A rock bounced off the tracks and struck Werner in the forehead as he heard a bunch of kids rejoicing on the opposite platform. It was the last sounds he heard as he fell off the tracks. Getting off his back, he pulled himself over the platform edge as the Manhattan-bound train on the opposite track departed. He stretched out on the platform with blood pouring down his nose but grateful he knew he would be okay. Two policemen came running towards him. The large Bulova clock said eight thirty-one. He blacked out. He dreamt of seeing a trailer alone on a mountain in a rural setting. Maybe there could be a nice future yet. He awoke in the hospital with Ida and his children, Frank and Joanie by his side. He was never to return to Bulova.

Werner went to a number of eye specialists but no one could bring back his facility for coordinated precision between his eyes and hands. He had to go out on Disability. The family's fortunes turned upside down. Ida went to work at the school cafeteria and the kids, Joan, age twelve and Frank, fourteen had to stay close to home when not in school. Werner remained at home and tried his hand at creating model cars, planes and trains for a while. He landed a steady account at a huge toy store in Jackson Heights, Queens called Gerstenhabers. The family eventually moved out of Babylon, Long Island and lived above a store in Jackson Heights. The subway traveled outdoors and ran all night over the apartment. The kids got used to the ruckus. The adults never did. This added tension to their lives. Kids would visit more and more to see the models before they arrived in the store. Werner became very beloved in the neighborhood. The twitch he had developed in his facial expressions were accepted and became part of his persona. The products he developed became the most important facet of the family's life.

The kids had status among their friends for the first time in their lives. Frank ran track at school and was beating kids two and three years older. Joan became interested in photography and went out to shoot pictures on weekends. She was a first-rate student. Ida never got over the railroad incident and the changes in her life. She had loved Babylon and being primarily a homemaker. She went from a part-time school cafeteria worker to a full -time waitress at Woolworth's food counter. Werner began to dream of having a laboratory for his models. He had his eye on a blue and white building on Roosevelt Avenue under the subway and across from Gerstenhabers. He spoke with the toy shop owners in his native German about his hopes and dreams. First, they laughed at his idea but as his inventory grew bigger, they started to listen.

Joan came home. She had won the science fair and also had one of her photographs appear in the school's paper. It was a shot of the

Goodyear blimp flying over Flushing Meadow Park, the site of the World's Fair a couple of years back. Frank had started to socialize with the neighborhood kids and attended what was called "gatherings". These were the first parties organized by the group. His shyness overcame his natural friendliness so he mainly observed the others. However, it was at one of these gatherings, that Frank heard of the mysterious shoemaker in the alley down the block from the Jackson Heights Castle building. This castle building had a legend of its own but the shoemaker escapade resembled the mysteries the kids were into during this time; the Hardy Boys mysteries. The boys in the neighborhood were following the sudden disappearance of the shoe heels discarded by the shoemaker in the alley. This paralleled the vanishing of the money raised by the milk money drive for the track meets against competing schools in other boroughs.

One constant link to both cases was the lack of a comprehensive investigation by any authority. The fact that these amateur sleuths were making connections between these two situations was most striking. Joan was brought into this project by Frank to take pictures and utilize her superior brainpower to aid the boys in their searches. She seemed to fit in fine and more than one boy began to crush on her as well. Frank had to play the part of the watchful and protective brother.

The headline in the school paper announced the kids' big discovery. SHOEMAKER ADMITS ROLE IN MILK BOX FRAUD! The attention grabber was the photograph of a flattened milk carton sandwiched between two planted shoe heels in a back room of the shoemaker's store. The photo credit was Joan's. But soon the kids were broken up in school by Frank moving on to high school and Joan still in middle school. Then the family received a break that would change their lives once again. Mr. Gerstenhaber of the toy store decided to rent the blue and white building under the subway to open up a new line of toys. The new line would feature primarily new models created by Werner. Ida was to work the register and Frank would stock the store when he was off from school and running track. The outside was decorated by photographs chosen by Joan with some taken by her. This annex to the big store was an entire family project with Werner making the models upstairs all day. The Model Shop was the new name of the annex. The whole community started to pay attention.

Things went on in this way for a few weeks. Ida suffered silently as the sound of the overhead subways played havoc with her nerves. She now heard the trains incessantly. Home, work it went on. Her nerves were in disarray. She offended Mr. Gerstenhaber on one of his visits accusing him of trying to drive her mad and his taking advantage of her family. He stormed upstairs and went up to see Werner, who apologized profusely. Meanwhile, Frank was on a skiing trip, a reward for winning the Math contest in school. He had become a Math and Science whiz. He did all the bookkeeping for the store and did all the pricing for the models. Joan was an award-winning photographer for many teen magazines and had a very uneasy relationship with her mother. She tried to give her mother solace but Ida did not receive it well. Joanie was the apple of Werner's eye. The store had been visited by Otto, the sinister shoemaker who had recently been released from prison. He stared at Ida for a long time and demanded to see the kids before a policeman shooed him out of the shop. This officer had taken to visit regularly. Gerstenhabers was putting up the Christmas lights on the avenue. They covered both sides of the street in front of their store and also the Model Shop. When Frank returned from his skiing trip, he had acquired a newfound maturity about him. His friends had helped him emerge out of his shell. All remarked on this. Werner glowed and tried to keep Ida from berating him as being too forward. Ida revealed to the family about Otto's visits and the effect it had on her. Frank nodded slowly. Werner hid behind his models. The Christmas lights brightened the platform covered street. The subway trains roared on. Otto hid outside the family's apartment in an alley. The weather got brutally colder.

Jackson Heights. It was nineteen hundred and sixty-nine.

Otto had an obsession with the family and soon both Frank and Joanie knew it. They knew from the case of the shoe heels in the alley what kind of creep Otto was. They worked with the area detectives to keep track of Otto bothering Ida. She had begun a relationship outside of her marriage with a teacher at PS 149 up on Thirty-fourth Avenue. He had come into the store to purchase some model airplanes for a nephew. His name was Ricardo and he was not as discreet as he should have been. Frank picked up on it quite quickly. He recorded a file on the frequent visits to the store and totaled up the clandestine meetings Ricardo had with Ida. Ricardo Baez was the full name and as Frank worked up the dossier, he noticed Otto lingering in the shadows as well. When he presented his findings to his father, Werner covered his eyes and his ears and buried himself in his work. Werner had made over two thousand models in the past three months. He had made lots of money but unfortunately, Otto was also aware of all developments romantic and monetary in the family.

Otto had developed a fixation where he believed he was Werner's double. Despite their German roots, there was no other detail that connected them except that they both loved Ida. However, Ida had moved on from Werner and was disgusted by Otto. The latter was blind to this rejection. He started having delusions that he was Ida's husband and that Frank and Joanie were continually plotting against him. He also harbored a deep grudge against the Gerstenhaber family. He had dumped a couple of shoe heels with dead animals attached to them in the alleys by their premises. He was planning a series of small robberies in both the toy store and the model shop hoping to frame Ida's lover Ricardo Baez. He started gloating about his endeavors in a luncheonette on eighty second street.

One person who showed an interest in Otto's ravings was an undercover policeman. Tommy Shaughnessy had worked with Frank and Joan on the case of the twisted shoemaker who turned out to be Otto. He had uncovered the evidence but did not testify in court, so therefore Otto did not recognize him. He had spent hours listening to Otto pine for Ida and plot against her. He had lent a sympathetic ear to Otto's hate-filled monologues against the Gerstenhaber family. He offered both goods and technical assistance to the volatile German establishing a toehold on the case. He worked studiously, bringing in countless pairs of shoes to be repaired by Otto. Eventually, Otto smelled a rat.

Otto accused Ricardo Baez of being a pedophile and gave Tommy dates, names and a brief lowdown of suspicious behavior chronicled in a dossier he had created. Tommy did not believe any of it but pretended to investigate Ricardo and stayed away from the luncheonette for a few weeks. Meanwhile, he was running a complete surveillance of Otto and his frequent visits to The Model Shop.

Woodstock had happened that previous Summer. The kids were in camps upstate and heard all about it but were both working and could not attempt to attend. Frank was a waiter at an upstate New York hotel. Joan doubled as a camp counselor and worked for the town newspaper as a photographer. This was in the Berkshires. This left Ida and Werner alone together at the Model Shop for too many hours. Otto entered the shop when it was closed. He sabotaged some kits leaving his wretched shoe heels in both the back room and the alley. Tommy Shaughnessy recorded all these moves. Ricardo Baez went to both Puerto Rico and Florida for the Summer. Frank was recruited by a millionaire at the hotel to do statistics as an intern for the upcoming school year. Joan did a major profile of a rock group from Chester, Massachusetts that played the Woodstock Festival. This pictorial was picked up by many music magazines and her future became bright. Tommy summoned Otto for questioning, secure enough in his findings to expose his cover and past connection to Otto. Ida attempted to run away which began a series of these attempts but returned to see Ricardo one more time who was still not in the area. Meanwhile, Werner fell into a long period of discontentment, not quite a depression but remained distraught for many years. He joined a tennis club in a nearby park and helped his spirits a little bit but ever so slowly. He pleaded with Ida to give the club a try but she wouldn't hear of it. He made a few friends, none of them Germans in the club. It would take years but he was slowly on the upswing from this point on. It was his first positive move in his personal life since the accident in Woodside.

Frank had a summer romance and after Woodstock, he started to moon a bit. The romance was coming to an end. Though it didn't feel like it was ending, he knew he would be starting college a year early and was given a chance to start a career in a very profitable business. The girl he was dating, Nina wanted to be a folk singer. She had made it to Woodstock and Frank had let her down. She was immensely inspired by the soft rock acts she had seen there like Crosby, Stills and Nash and Richie Havens. She was very into Joni Mitchell. She also liked James Taylor and Judy Collins. She felt that Frank and her were going in different directions, but he was such a caring guy. For a guy, that is. Nina had met his sister, Joanie that Summer and craved to be in their family. She hailed from Stony Brook on Long Island. Queens, to her, was a dark, striving place on the way to the big city. She especially was fond of the Village, both East and West. She thought she might move there in a couple of years or so and looked to getting a break playing in clubs down there. Frank was so smart, she believed he could help her to find her dream. But how could they remain together? Maybe Joanie could help her figure it all out. In fact, Frank told her that his sister could be brighter than him!

There was no better place for a child than a visit to Gerstenhabers' Toys. The bright fluorescent lamps highlighted rows of shelves filled with the latest playful inventions on the market. The most exciting gadgets, toys, games and dolls known to Man! Shiny firetrucks, fiery red with firefighters clad in the most striking of gear adorned with clangs, sirens and light. The effect, so real a simulation of what flew past in the dark, gray streets in Winter and late Fall. The sheer multitude of dolls displayed in such variety unlike any other store in Queens, possibly even Manhattan with the exception of FAO Schwartz. Department stores could not compete with the entire inventory of the Gerstenhabers' collections. People came from many areas to shop there. Children would rush in with their hearts aflutter and voices oozing with anticipation from many hours, days and weeks imagining this exciting day. Train sets with such abundance of tracks, parts and model representations that were housed in both Gerstenhabers' Toys and more in the Model Shop. Ingenuity on showcased display; all originals, military, construction, municipal services such as police, fire, ambulance, the many different vehicles and corps. Details, intricacies abound all due to the inventor Werner, a former watchmaker and repairman of major repute.

When the evening arrives, the children all departed with their treasures, there is a dimness of light that bathes the main store and its satellite store as well. Deep within the catacombs of the main store, Otto drags in his carcasses. They are the remnants of his shoe parts, especially, the shoe heels. He fills each of them with the gold and silver of past tragedies culled from another land not too long ago. Filled with madness of vengeance and not comprised of any shame, guilt and with no conscience, he unearths his tools of pitiful, pathetic infatuation with Ida onto the shelves and floor of the basement, the stock room. His vile demeanor speaks of the past and poisons the wonderful present with a trail of tears. Of buried horror and wicked in spirit. Surveilling this is Tommy Shaughnessey following this villain who travels by night, who foments evil in the darkness. Tommy builds his case, the greatest and most important of his life. With only thoughts of Justice, making sure his facts are in line with his hunches. Evidence is his only goal, to carry it to its natural conclusion. With all the finely tuned precision taught him by his trainers, he pursues the mission, the execution of the mission. He breathes in decency hoping to exhale the hatred that dwells in this violated space.

Chapter Two
"*CHICKEN*"

$\mathcal{Q}$ueens was the center of the universe in 1969. It was the year of the Mets, the Jets in Flushing. Woodstock was only two hours away. The Knicks would also win. For the kids so much hope and excitement hung in the air. The kids who threw the rock that hit Werner were living their lives in Jackson Heights. They were playing the Hardy Boys Mysteries in Otto's shoemaker's alley. Shaughnessy doing the same for real. Tommy had grown up at the Roosevelt Terrace complex off Thirty-seventh Avenue which is where Ida yearned to move her family. She wanted Ricardo Baez to use his influence in the neighborhood to get her on the waiting list. She had no inkling that Tommy had the history and connections need- ed to help her get on the top of the list. Their paths hadn't crossed at this time. Meanwhile, Otto was splitting his surveillance between the Model Shop and the Young Israel Synagogue on Thirty-seventh Avenue which was right by the Roosevelt Terrace. He lived in the old building that resembled a defunct castle on Eighty-ninth Street and Thirty-fourth Avenue, that is, when he chose to sleep at home rather than in the basement of the Model Shop or in alleys that he frequent- ed. The building was in disarray inside and its blue stucco veneer had turned into both purple and yellow in spots. Otto liked to spit on the lobby floor when entering to demonstrate his disgust. This was a world of contrasting emotions not far from the Miracle of the 1969 Mets and Jets. Shaughnessy himself was feeling like he was on a cloud due to the unforeseen victorious teams who had previously been the doormats of baseball and football, respectively.

Otto spat and stared malevolently at the street in front of his building. Ida cursed her husband, the Gerstenhabers and kept pursu- ing Ricardo to do things he just couldn't pull off. There was so much scheming, stalking, investigating amidst this excitement that permeated the neighborhood. Then tragedy struck.

There were a bunch of teenagers that hung out who lived at the Roosevelt Terrace complex. Periodically, they would play a game called "chicken" on the elevator cables. Ride up or down and jump off at the last floor before the cables would stop on either the roof or the basement. The guys were fifteen, sixteen or so and there were about ten of them who were part of the group. Tommy had caught them several times and got them to cut it out. Ricardo Baez knew most of them from elementary school and they were influenced by him as well. One night, two boys missed the jump off and fell to the bottom. Killed instantly. Tommy was on the scene almost immediately and assisted the police in gathering information. He helped clear out the congested and shocked crowd in the lobby. The surviving teens confided in Tommy and Ricardo. Otto passed through as well to receive whatever information he could collect to poison Ida later in her quest to move to the Terraces.

This became a traumatic memory for the many who were present and the rest of the community for about a week. The wreaths along Thirty-seventh Avenue seemed to weep. All kids big and small felt the cloud of mortality hover above them. Baez was on overtime to help the children and neighbors through this tragedy. Shaughnessy did an extensive study of the glue-sniffing habits of the local teenagers and concluded almost all were doing it and tried to counsel as many kids as he could. Both Frank and Joan stayed in their small circle of friends and their healthier pursuits to get through this period. Ida acted as if a ghost had infiltrated her hopes and dreams to destroy her move to Roosevelt Terrace. Werner disappeared so deep into his model-making he didn't even return home any longer. He preferred to sleep in the shop most nights. Haunted by the rock thrown on the railroad tracks, he slipped into nightmares of his youth and escape to America. He dreamed constantly of his childhood friends, especially Yakov and Chaim as he heard their voices warning him as the rock sailed through the air. Did they survive Germany? Are they alive somewhere? Are they perhaps in America, maybe Israel? How much he missed the fun of their youth before things turned into a nightmare. Poor Ida never forgot or forgave. He felt some forgiveness in his heart. Some. He had some for her straying, too. He knew it came from a long past wound. They both carried the ghosts of their families' past. Like unseen presences that followed their footsteps through this new world in Queens. Made them feel tired yet with a certain hope in the air. The sports affected everything in the borough. Lots of children had been born in the last ten to fifteen years. Werner saw them every day and they were poised for a better world. He rejoiced at having survived death in Europe. Ida, however, gravitated to the darker side as most with her background did. Werner was an exception. The rock adventure had awakened his miracle of surviving the camps. Ida saw it as a reminder of danger's omnipresence. The family would never be safe, never. The kids did not have the dark side, thanks to God. Frank wanted to solve the world's problems. Joanie sought out the world's wonder and documented it. They were both treasures! The neighborhood tragedy with those boys' glue-sniffing and deaths would teach all the kids not to take life so lightly. Ida just shook her head over and over and felt the Roosevelt Terrace apartments were ruined for her forever. Werner decided to take her on a carriage ride in Central Park for their twenty-fifth anniversary. Bring her back to show her the pure magic of the Gerstenhabers store. To look at it from a child's perspective. What a dazzling array of joy and light! Maybe Joanie could transmit the whole feel of it through her pictures. What an idea that was!

They only made it halfway on Werner's tour of the toy store. The first shelves all gussied up for Christmas had snow covered castles perfection. Multiple depictions of joyful domesticity of children in happy families complete with friendly pets and scenes of city grandeur and country bliss. Then moving on to cowboy and Indian games and costumes, guns, bows and arrows of distinct authenticity. Doll collections embodying all ages, hairstyles and costumes of the day to cast a spell upon all girls of different ages and backgrounds. Sporting goods unparalleled in volume. Bicycles and tricycles of all colors and containing all accessories. A space department with planetariums for rooms. There were space helmets, spacesuits as well as models of rockets, planets and other rotating spheres to capture all the sounds and shapes of space. Ida suddenly ran out in tears. Werner's spirit plummeted with his inability to please her so apparent. As Ida ran out of the store, a train's roar overhead rendered her hysterical. Otto and Werner then collided on the street and Tom witnessed the hostility between the men. It was like a blackout occurred for a second in Jackson Heights. Then the parties split up simultaneously, Werner back to the Model Shop, Otto to the alley behind Gerstenhabers, Tommy to the precinct to file his latest report. The late night fell and then the snow. Quiet resumed except the occasional train.

The kids were both deep on their ways. Joanie, lost in her photography. She hounded the New York galleries and helped out in a bunch of photo labs. Between school and volunteer work, she took multitudes of photos. Her camera was her constant companion. She had no time for anything else. Her friends missed her. Boys were off-limits and family life was a vortex of pain. Except for her father. She loved to use him as an example of productivity as he conceived his model kits. His happiness blossomed as he withdrew more and more from Ida. His love and pride in his children glowed within him. Frank was trailblazing a new direction in the music business. He ushered his girlfriend, Nina into the phenomenon of singer-songwriters. Starting in the Village and shuttling her into the Boston area with gigs and then out West in LA and San Francisco and all stops in between. Frank handled the publicity, advance work and yet kept up his studies with his goal of going to MIT on full scholarship. Jackson Heights grew tough and smart kids. He valued the vibe of Seventy-fourth Street and Eighty-second Streets. Music blared from the stores there. Nina would be another Joni Mitchell or Carole King. Frank worked the business from his room above the stores in Jackson Heights. Very close to the elevated subway. He caught a flash of Ida and her friend Mr. Baez of the elementary school from his window one night. Whatever floats your boat he said underneath his breath. His mother dragged down the old man who was lost in his work and his kids. It was ok, He guessed. The toy industry was a marvelous distraction. The corner of Jackson Heights with Gerstenhabers, The Model Shop and the Whistlestop Railroad Trains was flourishing and contributed greatly to the joy of the neighborhood. The numbers were there. But Otto's shadow did not escape him. He still worked with Tom Shaughnessy to rid the family of this evil character.

Otto plotted both day and night to bring down Baez, Werner and to drive Ida from her family. He planted various clues in the alleys around the stores as he used to do on Eighty-ninth Street. His inventory of vile artifacts housed in his shoe heels were kept in the wretched castle building a block away from his former shoemaker's shop. One morning Frank and Tom spied him in the alley marking boxes of pictures taken of Ida and Baez together. The pictures suggested that the couple had been in Mexico. Frank and Joan kept Werner sane through this onslaught. But the event made Werner even more of a recluse. Otto was brought in for questioning and charged for trespassing by Shaughnessy. Frank and Tom grew very close as did Joan and her father. Her photos were soon to be featured in a national magazine. She was working on a campaign of her father's model kits in print.

Then the kids who threw the rock in Woodside looked Werner up and everyone's life changed.

Chapter Three
"KICK OVER"

---

*O*tto Mertz liked to comb the streets of Jackson Heights. He searched for unclaimed treasures. He combed the beaches of Rockaway in the Summers. He enjoyed trading with other "underground" people. "Underground" meant to Otto, people that the normal people never noticed. They lived in hovels, alleys, basements, roofs, tracks, bridges and combed the streets for unclaimed valuables. Lockers, stations-bus and rail, airports, runways, train tracks, subway tunnels and bathrooms, under trestles which Queens was full of these trestles. He prowled the catacombs of society. He savored the tombs nestled among the living. Unnoticed by the living. He reviled in the dead relics coexisting with the meaningless drivel of real life. Which was the real deal? He wondered aloud as he wandered around. Otto prayed to nothing, no one. He cherished evil. He never forgot his debt to it. He plotted against his own corner of humanity. He was the world's refugee, after all. No one wanted him, if they really knew him. No one would want him if only…

He cashed in his chips to briefly become Otto the Shoemaker of Eighty-ninth Street and Northern Boulevard. There were four boys who had become fans of the Hardy Boys, the mystery series of the day. They chose to look in on Otto's strange endeavors and quirks. And he became aware of them immediately and surveilled their efforts. This is how Otto became aware of Werner Kaufman and his family. He linked these boys to Werner through the night at the Woodside station. These four boys were from scattered Jackson Heights areas. Three from the Seventies' blocks and one from above Ninetieth Street. Otto remembered the night that these four had dressed as cowboys one night and caught a subway at Woodside after a little horseplay below the subway at the Long Island Railroad Station. They went down to Times Square masquerading as visitors from Texas to gape at the tall buildings and make the people milling around look up at whatever they were marveling at. They put on a show for the locals in midtown Manhattan. Of course, before running up the stairs to get the subway, they committed a crime on the LIRR platform. They struck a stranger on the opposite side of the tracks with a rock and ran away in peals of laughter. Unbeknownst to them, there had been a witness to their caper. Otto Mertz. He had kept this bit of information under his hat as he recognized at least two of these boys and later identified the other two to a detective, Tom Shaughnessy, who Otto had never let on before that he knew Tom was indeed with the Police Department. It was worth relinquishing this knowledge to punish the boys for their crime. But through this revelation, Otto had found out that Werner was their victim. His next targets were the rest of the family and it was the secrets he harbored against all that were to set up all his activities for the next period of time. One day everything converged and only Tom Shaughnessy could connect all the dots. The boys, Werner, Ida, Frank and Joanie and Otto, the antagonist in this Jackson Heights tale. The trust between Tom, Frank and Joan would be tested throughout this ordeal. For as the boys played in the alley behind the shoe store, Otto was marking time to strike against them. The boys knew both Frank and Joan from school. Tom had to divulge he incident to the brother and sister who told Tom they were all good kids from good homes with life ambitions. Tom took them at their word and refocused his sights back on Otto. But Otto, started to torture the kids' parents with anonymous threats. He was becoming a huge nemesis in the neighborhood. And to add insult to injury, there was a common thread throughout his devilish actions. All the families he was bothering were all members of the same synagogue. Ida knew where this was going. She was a survivor of the camps. Her husband was a survivor of the camps. She dreamed about Otto and others she had encountered in her nightmares. She had these night-mares every night and Otto brought back the past and filled her with fear. Had she known him when she was a little girl? She started to convince herself that she had. She began to appear on the platform of the number seven subway train at Sixty-first Street in Woodside. One day she stuck her foot out as a small boy passed her. "Kick over", she muttered. She gave the mother of the boy a sick smile. The mother pulled her boy of seven back in an instant and went to complain to a subway policeman. Ida was questioned and arrested. She was released after a three day stay at the hospital for observation. Later on, she received a picture of dead Jews at a camp wrapped inside a shoe heel. Otto came into the store the next day and inquired if she had indeed received her "Linzer tart". She ran out of the store and disappeared through the subway turnstile. A few days later, she left the family. Tom later put together this progression of events. He knew it would be hard to find Ida. He would keep tabs on Baez but doubted she would remain attached to him after these assaults on her past. Frank and Joan devoted themselves to keep Werner intact. He fell into a deep depression stopping the model making and found a new interest; devising games. The trains rattled on above Gerstenhabers and the Model Shop. Also, in their apartment by the trains, they all remembered Ida's hatred of the noise. How she hated the store and didn't really want to be their mother or Werner's wife any longer. It was now just the three of them in this world of shadows of the past and the changing landscape of Queens and New York City. The bright futures of the kids and Werner's struggle to find a way to survive his plummeting feelings had to become the focus.

The unspeakable, unthinkable events in Werner's past, when he was an adolescent in Europe-no, the children were the only sunlight left in his world now. This had to eclipse his woe. Keep busy at all costs. He knew what was swirling around him but he did not recognize it consciously or he'd go under. Keeping busy was the key. He withdrew from peoples' lives including his own children, as he brought only darkness wherever he went. It was best to stand still and work. Let the children soar in what interested them. That made Werner feel good. He would never be an American father. Always a refugee who was spared and knew death on a first name basis and close up. Had only his little family left. He couldn't hold on too tight as it was so precious.

Max Sharansky was one of the boys at the railroad station the night Werner was felled by a rock. He was the chief architect of the Times Square Expedition. He posed as Lil Jake with big Rex Rothbaum as Big Jake. Billy Borowsky was the mischievous Rufus. The fourth member almost bailed before they started, Michael Oronoff known as Clem. Oronoff had white hair at age twelve from his penchant for worrying and high anxiety. He loved being the butt of the jokes. Three of these boys were to go on to the special high schools of New York City, meaning you had to pass an entrance exam. The schools were Stuyvesant in Manhattan and the Bronx School of Science. The only one who went to the neighborhood high school, Newtown was rocks in the head, Rex who wound up as a vocational placement early on in his high school years. If anyone was a prime suspect it would have been Rex. But the boys never really accepted that they had caused injury except for Max Sharansky. He wanted very much to apologize to Mr. Kaufman and pay for the crime but the others kept him from doing so for a while.

The boys went into Manhattan on the number seven train developing their characters and the mission on the fly. Both Max and Billy orchestrated the endeavor. Plotting the action and costuming the others in true technicolor Western apparel. Practicing the accents with Rex always threatening to break character and Oronoff fearing their exposure. He was in mortal fear of his father, a strict disciplinarian and fire department official. The only story the kids knew about Oronoff's father was one night he flushed his pajamas down the toilet after peeing in his sink. This fit with the son always being the butt of the others' jokes and his stance that his father was also a character. The show the boys put on in Times Square was the stuff of legends. They ran the streets like cowboys on the prairie and the people that witnessed it were treated to a live Western in the most crowded of streets. Lots of slapstick ensued. Rex and Max up-ended a chestnut cart and treated the crowds to free nuts. Clem and Rufus had a shootout around a taxi waiting for a light and so on. The police had to break up the act. When they took the train home, all red-faced and hoarse from whooping it up and laughing so much, they became subdued with the thought of what had happened with the rock. Max became fraught with guilt. Max was a lead organizer of the gatherings and the Hardy Boys adventures in the alley by the shoemaker. It was known that there had been a victim and Max thought he had seen a man rummaging through the station who might have seen them. It took quite a while until he found out the witness was Otto, the shoemaker. But Max wanted to know had any of the boys actually thrown the rock. When did it happen? In their brief discussions of the matter, no one took ownership of the deed. Then they changed the subject. But Max became doubtful that it was any of the boys that did it. They were all wrapped up in the show they were going to put on. As Otto became discovered as the fiend that he was, Max began to think it was him who had thrown the rock and was trying to pin it on he and his friends. It was Otto who found the rock with Mr. Kaufman's blood on it and it was Otto who led the police to it and the fact that the boys were there. Max and Frank had become close and Tom soon saw that the boys were being played and worked with them to get more and more evidence against Otto. Meanwhile, Max had several reasons to want to meet with Mr. Kaufman. He was carrying quite a torch for Joan Kaufman, but would not tell the other boys about it. He brought Frank into the shoemaker's alley mysteries and Frank brought Joan to do the pictures. Max was observing and helping her through her tasks. It was his chance to see her out of school. But when Joanie found out that the boys were connected to the rock, even though Frank had cleared them with Tom, she shunned Max anyway. She did file the cowboy show at Times Square an interesting feather in his cap but for the time being he was off limits to her. Rex eventually tried to take matters in his own hands regarding Otto but Tom stopped his revenge plan. Eventually, Joan started to thaw out about Max' role with the rock and soon her, Frank and Max became very close and Max met Werner and became like one of the family.

So, all these wires and stories converged. Everyone in the story was linked up. Ida soon disappeared and Otto's real plans were to be revealed.

Chapter Four
DEPARTURES

---

*I*n a very small town in Ohio, a middle-aged woman with a European accent arrived one day and moved into a three-room apartment above a grocery store. She took a job in the town's laundromat. She gave everyone the same unfriendly look. A look filled with suspicion. She had left her husband and family. She went under the name; Ina Coffman. The husband she had no more feeling for. She missed her son for he figured out so many things. Not her girl who was too headstrong for her own good. These children would be all right. They had brains and talent. The husband she left was too preoccupied in his models, his creations to even think of her and her complaints. Her moods would not affect anyone else now. She could walk out of the town and see cows, horses and sheep like she did when she was a girl. So long ago. If she was in a bad mood, she could glare at the customers. The days passed fast enough.

One day she had an idea. The man, whose secret only she knew would never give anyone in her family any peace of mind unless she left and could lure him away to follow her. She waited for the day when he would also arrive in the town. She would live this solitary life and cherish the peacefulness she could never have under that subway and its noise. It only reminded her of the cattle cars and Jew Hatred she escaped. The peace of her little apartment held her together. She cried a little about what she had left behind but continued on with her steely resolve to do what was necessary. Anonymously, in this forgotten town. A little spot in the godforsaken universe. Jew Hatred had robbed her of her soul. Her hope. Her softness. Her humanity. Survival became all encompassing. First in the Old World and now in the new one. But in looking forward, it would end away from her family. It must be so. Her husband was really now her former husband. Too soft, too broken and consumed with his busy hands to even see what things were about. Werner was an island to himself. She had her Latin lover until she could regain her mind. She flooded her senses and then she found her center once again. Frank and Joanie would become free of what took her soul away. She was to see to it.

Her first pang began. It was about her youngest, Joanie. Her brave little one. She would look at the world through her many lenses. Maybe, make it a little more beautiful and hopeful. But also she would come upon the most brutal of images. There would be no escaping that. How she wished she could spare her that. As her world turned like the fourteen washers and dryers she supervised, she would suddenly see Joanie's face. It would call to her, " mother, mother where are you? Why did you leave us?" Avinu Malkenu, my dear daughter I have to do something for God, our King. Please forgive me. I see the girls come down Main Street, your age with their energy and I think of your fierceness, my darling. Then the pain stopped for a while. Then it started again about the boy, Frank. So brilliant, so helpful, so good-hearted but so innocent like his father, Werner. The husband she stopped pretending to love. But Frank, she missed with such pitiless darkness. The boy would amaze the world with his sharp mind. Save many people with his ingenuity. As long as he doesn't fall for faithless women like his mother. As long as he is not taken by the swindlers of the world. That someone powerful would see to it that Frank would be a valuable cog in a worthwhile enterprise. An argument started in the laundry and she had to get between the quarreling yokels. Ach, stuck in this Ohio until her business was done. The Almighty placed her there for a purpose. The end would come there when the deed was done.

The same dream every night. A sour man searching through the underwears of the captives. A camp surrounded by barbed wire. They were penned in like cattle. And this sallow, sullen man took his time examining the women. He took their possessions and very fondly touched their underwears. He combed around their beds with his eyes darting over them, snickering, muttering to himself. Laughing and enjoying their fear and suffering. Taking the soles out of their shoes. She never forgot that and stuffing these soles into his pockets as he shuffled out until the next day. It would begin again and at night the same routine ensued. If he caught one observing his actions, he would point and others would come and take the woman away, most never to return, others brought back with no life left in their beings. He was known to all as the German Termite. He fed on both their souls and their bodies. How he came to be in the same place as Ida's family in America was a tragedy. He fixated on her like the insect he was but to see him in action once again on the survivors in this new world, on the children of those that survived, no she would rather die than witness this obscenity.

The little town in Ohio had a festival in the Fall. Before the town disappeared into its wintry chill, suspended into a cold freeze of three, four brutal months of oblivion. Hibernating with the animals. Then to emerge in the Spring, coming out of their homes, rubbing their eyes and greeting each other again like long lost travelers. Before all of this, Ina Coffman attended the Fall Festival, starting out sticking by herself as the stranger she was. A shadow from the laundromat, who gave change, folded clothes and kept order in her anonymity awakened when she heard the music and dancing that began in the town's Grange Hall. She proceeded to dance with many men, laughed and socialized unlike any other time in her recent past. She almost forgot herself in her merriment. Almost, but not quite.

And Joanie woke up. Her mother had left her, it was true. Her brother Frank and her had to be the parents now, the father like a son. She couldn't even ponder the thought of looking for her mother. Good riddance! She brought them down with her scowling and self-ish ways. It was horrible to think that of your own mother but now the three of them could finally breathe. The mother was only committed to knocking the starch out of them. An endless river of self-pity and a sorrowful, bitter outlook of the world that dealt millions a harsh blow, not just her. She never could see that side. Never. And yet, Joanie kept looking at the world with color and light. A breeziness of hope. A smile. Musical reflection. Good riddance to everlasting clouds and moping. But she did feel a little like an orphan.

Seventy miles south of Cincinnati, a man walked slowly down a road. He was on his way to a small town. In his pocket he carried shoe leather cutouts. He had a picture of what he'd be doing when he reached his destination. He gnashed his teeth with each step. "Thought she'd get away from me". He trudged along the highway, lights beamed from the oncoming traffic. One step at a time, his beaten face not seen by the glare. A beating that Tommy Shaughnessy had given him on the way to being dumped in the hills of Pennsylvania after Shaughnessy had read him his crimes. After Shaughnessy revealed Otto's pattern of harming people from his days living in Jackson Heights. "I'm doing the neighborhood a service. I'm performing a mitzvah for the Jews, as they say. I'm doing all people an honor by throwing a piece of garbage on the fruited plain. He drove off, choking dust falling on Otto Mertz, hobbling along the desolate road. Otto's mind still filled with undeterred evil that would become someone else's nightmares. Curses instead of prayers, grimacing with pain, finding his path to more destruction paved with glowing coals of unrepentant ill wishes. Hurtling through the night.

Werner made his twenty-fifth box of model airplanes for the week. He stood up from his work table. He stretched his weary arms. He called out to his daughter. And he dropped dead.

Chapter Five
SEPARATE JOURNEY

Two separate journeys were taking place. Ahead was Joanie by about two days. Behind were Max Sharansky and Frank. All going to find Ida in Ohio. They all had a vague idea where she was. A small town named Zevron. Somewhere south of Cincinnati. A town of farms or a farm town whatever they called it over there. The kids didn't really know. Max and Joan had begun hanging out in Queens and were at this point inseparable except for this trip. Some friends called them insufferably inseparable. Max liked to invent scenes and Joanie liked to take pictures. They were two creative young people with boundless energy and imagination. They found great humor in the smallest things and wonder in all natural occurrences. They also liked travel and didn't want to be tied down. Joan's idea was to get Ida back home where her and Frank were coping with their father's death and their mother's disappearance. Frank was keeping his sister and himself afloat by working after school and marketing his father's numerous creations and Joan had been pressed into service doing print media. Max was helping them by creating ads for their father's store to stay open. Ida was needed back there but her sanity had to return first and this could be a tall order. All hands were needed for that.

Max loved the way Joanie would say his name. Max was becoming part of the Kaufman family. He was like a new Kaufman. Tom Shaughnessy had kept the secret of Max and his friends being involved at the railroad tracks rock incident. Max himself had been struck by a rock in the third grade before his family moved to Jackson Heights. He just knew that they had all been innocent in the Bulova tragedy. He was ready to nail Otto Mertz on that incident and the ones in the alley as well. Frank had gotten him wise to all the intricacies and meanwhile Max had completely fallen for his sister. He went nuts at her just saying his name. He went crazy at her eyes capturing wherever they would be. Her brain, spirit, her looks had him over the moon. He'd never felt this way before. Max Sharansky was known as the hippest kid around and yet his cool was no match for the feelings, he found he had about her. He was totally at her beck and call. He would get Ida back to Queens if it made Joan happy. Max had never known how to be for anyone other than for Max. People were amazed at the change. Joanie understood it for what it was. "Max", she uttered repeatedly, positioning him for some grand scheme to find and entrap her mother to do the right thing for once. To restore her sanity and maternal feelings, to overcome whatever plagued her for most of Joan's life. Frank had prepared Max for all contingencies. Joan snapped picture after picture as she journeyed alone while Max and Frank went over their plans. The element of surprise was the key to their success. Ida would be tough to fool, always on her guard. She was surely a survivor. Max's real family had also had their share of Holocaust survivors. He knew the atmosphere of always identifying the escape route in all situations. He was brought up too, in that environment. Joan and Frank had tried to ignore these impulses, to rise above it. Max had bought it as a philosophy much more than the Kaufman children. Those instincts were burrowed deep in his gut. He thought of Joan once again, his heart bursting with understanding. We will succeed, I promise, he muttered under his breath. His body shook with expectation, his reflexes on high alert. Frank and Max travelled on in the dark now. Miles closer to Ohio.

Frank Kaufman and Max Sharansky had formed a friendship one day in Middle School after years of mutual indifference. What had drawn them together was a scene created by Max at a "gathering" where a boy put on a performance to woo a girl to go on a date with him. The crux of the drama was the pretension of being a chronic wallflower and transforming into a wild uninhibited dancer and twirling the girl around. All of this developing from the adrenalin of fearing being turned down. Precision and conviction were executed in such a way that Frank was astonished by the feat. The trust that Max had infused his corps so completely bemused Frank to no end. He was impressed to say the least. Frank identified with this wallflower persona yet yearned to a great extent to let out his alter ego. He followed Max out of the social get together and questioned him about every detail of the performance. They wound up palling around the rest of the school year. When Max visited Frank at home, he laid his eyes on his sister and vice versa and the rest has already been recounted. At times, they were like a trio of adventurers pushing each other's creativity, originality and intelligence to terrific levels.

They loved to go to LaGuardia Airport and pretend they were each taking off on an unknown trip. Emotions would swell to great levels and crowds would gather at the display of such emotions. The sorrows and the fierceness of hugs and embraces. For Max, these expeditions rivaled the cowboys in Times Square. He had a new part-ner Frank, and they would brainstorm scenarios to do away with the evil Otto Mertz. The hero worship of Tommy Shaughnessy. The decency and skill of Werner Kaufman. The easing of pain and bit-terness for Ida Kaufman. The grandness of the spectacle that was the Gerstenhabers' Toy Store. The nobility of the neighborhood in Jackson Heights, Queens. The glory of youth, the hopefulness, the eagerness to explore, the inquisitive nature of all three youngsters. All in their most awakened state. It was a celebration! Others in their circle marveled at their coordination of activity. As if they were unleashed on the world to do good, expose its darkness and reveal its goodness.

Then Ida left and then Werner dropped dead.

But Frank was now on the trail of Otto. Otto was to blame for the downward spiral of his family. The true cause. Without Otto, his family would still be together, Werner alive. He had gone over this with Max a thousand times. Max had had his own run-ins with the shoemaker. Max had also witnessed a vile demonstration of Otto following Ida and her fear of him. Her face had visibly turned ashen. Then she yelled at him in an imperious tone. It had seemed very strange and sent chills up his spine. "Let's do something, Max", Frank said one day. And soon it began that they were on their way to Ohio right behind Joanie.

The shoe heels in the alley had been fully revealed by Tom Shaughnessy. Whoever was targeted by Otto had something precious stolen and these items were sewn into a shoe heel. The more personal they were, the more precious to Otto's way of thinking. A collection of artifacts which brought immediate heartache to those they originally belonged to. Like a messenger of Death or a souvenir seeker of forgotten veils of tears, Otto arrived, delivered sorrow and moved on. He particularly picked on Holocaust survivors. This predilection threatened his own freedom but he could care less. To inflict pain and suffering to his former victims was all he cared about. Tom Shaughnessy had been dedicated to stopping the heartbreak in Jackson Heights yet Otto constantly got sprung to continue doling out this vicious salute to the defamed who survived. These reminders were so premeditated and hateful that even though Tom had no familial connection to the victims, his human connection commanded him to get Otto off the streets. His last attempt was to beat and chase Otto out of Queens and into the midwestern fields of Ohio.

Otto, who had just about been left for dead, woke up and continued on to Ohio. Muttering to himself, bleeding and functionally scrambled, he still was on his way to execute his plan. Equipped with heels loaded up with precious memories, designed for Ida Kaufman, he trudged onward one painful step at a time. He constantly looked back over his shoulder. He was warily devoted to his own survival. He edged into the alternately warm and cold night. While two boys kept a close distance behind. All three young people on their way with great hopes for a successful resolution. Catching the moonlight through the storm's breaks, the sounds of the Saturday night festivities growing louder in the distance. This was where Ida had just made a hasty retreat after wowing the townspeople with her life of the party dancing. Otto, gasping like a dying horse. Ida's hoarse laughter hanging in the Ohio air amid great wind and weather. Summer being chased out into mid-Fall in one fell swoop.

Ida had danced feverishly at the Grange Dance. She left quickly as a middle-aged man was in pursuit of her all night. After her fifth dance with him, she was feeling both excited and crazed. This violated her overall plan. She started planning her escape through two streets and up a winding staircase. Charles, the man she danced with, anticipated her moves and waited outside before she fled. He wound up walking her home. She was polite but refused his advances. She agreed in a few days to meet for coffee and let him kiss her goodnight. She ran up the steps and took a deep breath of relief. She turned on her light and Joanie jumped up from the bed. "Ach, you gave me a scare, Joanie, what are you doing here?". "Daddy's dead, Mama, you left us. Come back with me". "Never". Ida replied, "We discuss tomorrow. I'm tired". She had shown no emotion so Joan said. "What kind of monster, are you?" "You know nothing. Go to sleep.", answered Ida and turned the lights off.

Max and Frank were two days behind. So inseparable were Max and Joan, it felt to them that they were on the road together. Otto had flagged a ride to the town. A doctor had cleaned him up and treated his wounds. Otto heard the music at the Grange. He went up to the place the music came from about eighty minutes after Ida had left. He started asking the people there about the funny German lady and soon learned of her living arrangements and her job in town. However, his queries attracted the attention of Lt. Bruce Sherman, who came over to the town clerk Mary Donovan and began to question the German refugee himself. He asked about Otto's beating, dishevelment and all around slovenly appearance. "Why are you so far from New York and what brings you to our town? Why are you so interested in Ina Coffman?" and so on. Otto answered flawlessly that they were cousins and was offered shelter by the town's selectman. Otto declined, ran away and found a hiding place in the brush. It was almost Harvest Time and he prepared a few shoe heels for his most important visit. He then closed the slits that served as his eyes and dreamt his most evil dreams. The boys were only a few miles back and breathing hard. Nervous. Max dreamed of Joan. His thoughts were concerned with the state of her mind. Frank dreamed of his father. A good man. A nice man, both damaged and pure. His father was gone for good. Could they save his mother? God, could they save his mother?

Chapter Six
LIFE CAN GO ON

---

*O*tto crawled next to the railroad tracks in town following Frank and Max to the depot in the center of town. Otto had stopped by the toy store in town earlier, peeked into the window and made a mental note to return after dark. He had an idea to furnish some shoe heels with fillets of doll parts to make them appear more German. He had also stopped by the local delicatessen. He ordered franks loaded with sauerkraut and some very strong garlic pickles. Bopping into the local pharmacy, he sought out drops which paralyze a victim for hours, which he had secured a prescription prior to his journey. When the kind man behind the counter checked with his doctor, Otto beat it out the door with the drops. He then froze on the curb as he spied Ida staring at him. She pointed and screamed and Otto ran the other direction and landed on Frank's car. Max jumped out and pinned him down. Otto took a deep breath, opened his mouth and shocked Max with his severe garlic smell and grabbed the paralyzing drops and put them into Max's open mouth. He then ran straight into Ida's arms. She choked him and then clocked him. Frank grabbed Ida and brought her to a safe place. Joan ran up shouting, "I got it all on film!"

As Otto recovered in the Ohio hospital the authorities went through his possessions and found trinkets of many Holocaust survivors and victims who died in the concentration camps. Otto had collected them over the years and was going to present them to his many targets to counteract the loss of Germany in WW11. He despised living in the United States and cared only to trumpet his vicious plans of revenge on both survivors and their families. Thus ended his time as the ghost of a neighborhood, a toy store and especially, a once peaceful and loving family.

Max Sharansky dedicated his adult life to prosecuting war criminals as an attorney for both the US Government and then the Simon Wiesenthal Center. Joan had a tempestuous love affair with Max through their late twenties and early thirties but her photo assignments all over the world took their toll on their relationship. She had changed her name to Joey Skye and Max pined after her for many years after they broke up.

Frank Kaufman was a genius on Wall Street and show business. He served on many financial boards and capitalized many worldwide creative and humanitarian projects.

Ida found a way to travel extensively and kept track of the children from afar. She had accomplished her mission. She avoided eye contact with strangers. Every time she knew of a dance, she would rush to participate alone. She would slip out before anyone could get to know her.

Chapter Seven

1992 / CONNECTING THE DOTS

---

*M*ax Sharansky had been summoned to the office of the
United State Attorney for War Criminals in Washington
D.C. This was in 1992. A discovery had been made regarding former
Nazis who trafficked in the selling of smuggled mementoes of Holocaust victims. "Max, does the name Otto Mertz, ring any bells for
you?", his boss asked. "Years ago, when I was a teenager friends and
I stopped this man from harassing relatives and other survivors in
Queens, NY. We turned him into the authorities in Ohio". The boss
responded, "Well, Tom Shaughnessy, special agent, has requested
you specifically to join him in prosecuting Mertz". "It would be my
pleasure to see and work with Tom again." Tom and Max proceeded
to prepare the case. Otto had taken to lying in a fetal position and
bellowing in German his view of his own superiority to all living
creatures. Singling out the Jews as particularly low. All the filthy vows
of the Third Reich came out of his mouth in a full German sneer. It
was otherworldly to bear witness to this. He was devoid of any real
consciousness in the real world and dwelled in his memory's hole
buried deep somewhere below the ground. It was only in this hole
could he focus his attention. The facts, the evidence of the case elud-
ed his comprehension. His presence was waived and his defense team
could not reach where his mind had relocated to. This was a very
dark business Tom and Max had to practice in. Things moved very
slowly as Otto's state of mind was carefully determined. Even if it was
an act couched in cowardice, legal protections were strictly enforced.
It proved to be a demoralizing experience for the prosecution. Otto's
state of mind, the facts, the damage to the victims, the past indigni-
ties to the Jewish victims, all this inhumanity protected by humanity's laws. Max needed to leave rooms repeatedly.

Around the halfway point of the legal proceedings, Frank Kaufman had bankrolled a national exhibit of photography against Jewry rephotographed with commentary and curated by his sister, Joey Skye. Joey came to Washington to present this exhibit. The whole art world was taken aback by the depiction of savagery by both the Nazis and also Otto Mertz photographed in both his youth and later on in America doing his ugly deeds. A monstrous sneering Otto was the central photo in the entire exhibition and fueled the promotion of this nationally covered show. The public was infuriated by the image. Joey was accompanied by her newly reunited mother Ida who had been found wandering the streets of San Francisco. She had been tabbed the Barbary Coast Dancing Witch. Her angry demeanor amidst her life of the party actions brought her this notoriety. Homeless, cultured women were still a novelty at this time. Joey had seen herself through a very extended battle to get Ida in her custody. Though Joey possessed great compassion, she had been sorely tested by her mother to achieve this custody. It was an unrepentant world to Ida, she neither forget nor forgive. She had become barely recognizable to her daughter and Ida felt nothing for her children or the past life she had lived back in Jackson Heights. Like Otto, she had crossed into a land that was forever estranged from reality.

The reunion of Joey and Max was incredibly charged. Their last break-up was extremely volatile. Joey had dived into a period of work, so deeply personal and self-punishing she thought she would disappear permanently from society. Max had transferred his disappointment into catching and prosecuting the world's worst criminals. His pursuit of such inhumane souls was accomplished through such prowess his record was unmatched by any other Nazi prosecutor. But it had taken such a toll that inside he was split as the two lovers had once been so inseparably entangled. And now here they were, entwined in such interpersonal and inescapable involvement. They were the messengers to the world of both justice and the documented suffering of their people.

Chapter Eight
JOEY

Joey Skye was a fictional character that came from the mind of Joan Kaufman of Jackson Heights, Queens. A stunning beauty with light brown hair and a penetrating stare out at the world that always amazed her. She had been in the limelight as a celebrity photographer for over twenty years. She loved travel and photographing details and the changes within the details. She loved capturing people, houses, landscapes and urban scenes, basically anything to alert the world of the unusual. She was the eyes of the world. A far-seeing soul, a poet of the visual. A teller of the truth she sought. She possessed the detailed mind of her father and the irreverent passion of her mother. She hung out with the cool kids in the neighborhood and when she grew up, she hung out with the movers and shakers on both coasts. She was comfortable in whatever scenes she was documenting for big name print media.

But she never got over her high school crush, Max Sharansky. He had the attention of the schoolyard. He could create scenes with other kids that screamed, "look at me, Joanie!". "Join me and let's make our world together." When she was with Max, they were so wrapped up in each other, eventually, she couldn't breathe. She could lose herself in him but he had no fear of losing himself in her. This helped her run when the world came calling. She fled to Los Angeles and became the invented Joey Skye and made all the front covers with her photos. Max, on the other hand, sought out the darkness with his law degree and sense of justice. His legacy became all important. To preserve his race for his Holocaust survivor parents Sol and Eva Sharansky. They clung to their religion like it was a life raft during the Sixties and Seventies. Max instead relied on the imagination he had used against Otto Mertz as a teenager to succeed as a Nazi hunter. He later determined that Otto had been the rock thrower in Woodside that had struck Joanie's father through his relentless problem- solving skills. But alas, when it came to emotions, Max was as lost as the next man. And Joanie had his number for sure.

Now it was coming together again. Max prosecuting Otto. Joey on page one. Boy, this was going to be tough! The first thing Otto demanded when he was brought back to his senses by medication, was his old shoemaker's bag and his materials. He started planning a present for Max Sharansky. It was a rock made of clay, a skull made of porcelain and a silhouette of a beautiful girl cut out of leather. The nhe laughed maniacally in his cell until Max was summoned when he gave him these items. He wanted Max to remember that he and he alone, Otto Mertz knew all the keys to the Kaufman's misfortunes. He let Max know he was a co-conspirator. Max, by this time has been so versed to these Nazi tricks, he was immune to this attempt as well. However, because Joey was involved, he was curious where Otto was going. He kept presenting Max with larger and larger silhouettes of Joey and the rocks with busts of Werner and Ida. Joey finally came to Otto's cell. She snapped close-ups of Otto's eyes, closer and closer highlighting the depth and hollow darkness that even Otto had to finally look away and resist any more pictures. He cried out," leave me, leave me". And so, this game ended. Then Joey regaled him with stories of her happiness of reuniting with her mother. Her mother's progress and how she was hoping that Max and her would get back together and create many Jewish offspring. Otto crumpled again into a fetal ball.

Otto was soon found guilty of war crimes and subsequent peace-time crimes as well in America and sentenced to life imprisonment in a prison on the West Coast. Max and Joey had been seeing each other again and were facing a bright future again together.

Chapter Nine
A NEW STRUGGLE

So, this once hippie chick who traipsed through the end of the Sixties and beginning of the Seventies making her way through the rock world, the drug culture and back to the East Coast from the West Coast for the Eighties. Her fame expanding throughout all of the arts. Her photography resonating through the different scenes, periods, locations and finally leading to stunning portraits of the famous. Her incandescence and leadership as well as mentorship of the many artists and medias that arose through the years cemented her as a leading innovator and commentator of her time. She wound up exhausted and stuck creatively, again meeting Max and creating a child with him as well as recreating the enormous flames of their love once again until she had to flee once again.

Her reemergence to the world this time completely finding a new source of vision and a change of vibe, washing out of her that man and his relentless search for justice and the world's redemption. Only her art would suffice in her new world. A lighter vein would have to be found and a new life in the countryside for her daughter and herself. The new family of the two of them to assuage the forgotten mother who left her behind. Great gigs again and fabulous respect but always putting the fact that she was now a single mother with a home to return to.

Then the Ida, Otto, and Max show once again upsets the apple cart. The family now again in the public eye and the hero of this movie is Max. The hero of her movie is always Max. Can she dare risk showing this again? In memory of her dead father and to honor her wonderful brother she again commits to help. She falls under their protection again; Max and Frank.

The victimhood at the hands of this vile monster from the Holocaust. Max, the Jew in white knighthood yet all she wants is to keep her life away from this romance that ends, resumes, ends again twisting through her charmed life and then mixes with the old, helpless life of her youth. "Yes, Max, I'll help any way I can, of course". Will the door reopen with loss of privacy, feeling the remorse, the familiar regret the path that ends in a volcanic passion blown asunder. "Yes, Max, I'll be yours, again".

Chapter Ten
MAX AND A VISION

---

*I*t all comes down to timing. The recognition of seizing the right moment to fight with all of the soul to achieve one's destiny. To subside the fears and quell the doubts. To stem the tide of derision and make the difficult possible. Max, after all, was a master of timing. The realms of empowering the victims, pouncing on a jury and creating a scene in court that is most potent. This was his specialty. But to finally win Joey. Never had it been easy to find the right timing to make it their destiny. To make them realize their destiny. Just temporary sparks. It was now the time to utilize all his guile, knowledge and yes, opportunism if necessary to finally achieve his goal. He had given this great thought since their last break-up and then finding out about the little girl. He wanted to be with them both more than anything he had ever done.

He had hatched a plan for this occasion. He would re-create the Gerstenhaber spectacular exhibit to spellbind both the mother and child. The visual splendor he wanted to create would have to match the emotional wealth he possessed in his heart for the two of them. He would not rest until this was done. It must appeal to all the artistic and noble sensibilities she had deep inside her core. The images must capture both her heart and mind. For she could not forsake her love again. He couldn't survive another loss of both of them. This now became his sole passion, dream and vision and his objectives had been fueled for years. To once again the inseparable state they once had. He had to overcome her resistance.

Joey rejected her mother for good for many years after the Ohio adventure. But she had to save her mother right before the trial and she had escaped Max twice before after a closeness she knew deep inside she could never have with anyone else. During the trial,

Max had planned to bring Joey back to Jackson Heights when the verdict was coming down to the conclusion and win her back for the final time. Frank was wise to this as well and counselled his sister that it was best for Joey and the girl, Hannah to reunite with Max for good and ride out the combustible nature of their relationship and for once, stay together. Joey's head disagreed while in her heart, things were not so simple. Max had painstakingly done his homework. He had completely researched the Gerstenhaber plans for their spectacular exhibits. He had reached out to many of these collaborators of the Gerstenhabers' and newly recommended artists to bring back this reproduction. It was to be housed in a loft building in the old neighborhood halfway between where Joey and Max had grown up. Max presented this reproduction the night after Max was found guilty of war crimes and further crimes in America. The exhibit began with tall columns leading up to a sky ceiling of blue umbrellas. They were opened up to reveal angels with kaleidoscope faces. Into the foyer, one was accompanied by electric trains steaming through towns of New England architecture ringed around by placed green pastures with livestock roaming. The rooms situated further in were populated by blue ocean strips of golden beaches on one side and candy-coated brown mountains all under celestial skies. This all thundered amidst shooting comets. There were rooms of every doll imaginable for the five-year-old Hannah to see. Finally, there were walls covered by every photo ever published and every story covered by Joey in her career. A celebration of sound and color of joyous images a little girl could want for Hannah. Clouds of all shapes and sizes spelled out "My Only Dream is to be with Both of You".

Joey was so moved and confused she slapped Max in the face and ran away. Her emotions were overflowing and uncontrollable.

Chapter Eleven
THE FINAL MILE

———————————————

*M*ax waited and waited for an answer from Joey. No word from her. None came. She had left for London for a show. Before she left, she had gotten the manager of the building that used to be Gerstenhabers to open it for her. She spent many hours in the deserted space contemplating her life, her relationships, her feelings as an artist, as a mother and as a person, most of all in the darkness of where she spent many hours of her youth. She photographed the barren space for her own reference and thought of Max' recreation in the loft. She felt only a yearning of what, she couldn't yet place it.

Max just kept waiting. He didn't eat or sleep much. He suspended his activities in court and in the hunt for his people's enemies. No concentration for it anymore. It was time to either start living or just...he didn't know. A whole year had gone by. He packed his car to go West. He thought he'd just get lost out there. No more purpose. A life with no purpose. He had never had this but this seemed to be his future now. With his spirit hanging low to the ground, he started the car. Closed his eyes. Opened them put the car into drive and...

A welcome sight appeared. A beautiful woman with a beautiful spirit with a beautiful six-year-old daughter. The girl held something in her hand. It was a flower with a picture of a rainbow in her other hand. She held out the rainbow to Max. The sun was shining brightly.

WHEW!

*R*obert got into the vehicle he'd pined for all his adult life. He was soaking up his new surroundings. It was like driving around in a movie, a Western It was in the hills of southwestern Virginia. Green hills, meadows, pastures with mountains in the distance everywhere he looked. A bright, yet constantly changing sky. For a boy from Queens, New York, this was a foreign paradise. Up from misery, hopelessness, breakdowns, even. A long time of these. He felt re-energized, thrilled even though he was entering old age. He had achieved his lifetime dreams-house, environment, inner peace, comfort within, children were ok, women he loved at peace, happy, happy. Ok with religion, though distant from it. Spirituality intact. Health seriously compromised but feeling great. Exercising daily, eating well, taking good care of himself since he had recovered from the depths of despair. He had risen up from it all. Ghosts retreated far into the background. Still able to encounter new ones, however. This drive was fantastic! And best yet, endlessly available. This inner peace so valiantly fought for. He whooped in the car and almost drove off the road. Whew!

Robert didn't know a soul in Virginia. He had left New York in triumphant fashion. There was a dinner held in his honor. People respected his station in life. He'd touched their lives and they touched his. However, he was on his way out of town to start anew. He had stayed in one place for around twenty years and it was time to leave. Time to re-awaken these old bones and re-start the battery. He felt it deep in his soul. He needed to sort things out and get out into the country. Feel the wind rustling through the trees. Hear the whistle of it, too. He wanted a moderate temperature. Enough with the extremes. He took a breath and stopped to look over a ravine. He started walking and didn't stop until he realized he could get lost. Something was occurring to him now. Pictures of places, images of people and scenes from the past. Feelings started to come up. He almost blacked out. Stopped. Regrouped. Resumed and got back to the car before it got dark. Enough excitement for a day. Went back home and marveled at the sunset from his deck. Day one gone.

A week later and Robert did his first gig in a bookstore. Takes a chance. Signs books but reads from only new pieces. Since the old ones are brimming with Northeastern ideas, he is perturbed that they may induce culture shock in his new surroundings. He finds that he need not worry. He gets up on the rostrum and reads from "Walking from Oblivion". As he begins, a woman shouts out "I know where you're coming from, Char-lie".

Afterwards, he finds a diner near the bookstore called the Virginia Diner. It was one of the only diners he'd seen in Virginia. He looks around. He sees a few old boys talking to each other. They nod to Robert as he steps in. There are a few women as well. They are friendly, too. Everyone is friendly in this part of Virginia. There was an old boy holding court at the counter. His name was Guy. He was a mechanic and he was also a fiddle player. He seemed inebriated but he was recounting stories of what he called the Ridge in a straightforward way. The Ridge was on a mountain overlooking the town. He was telling stories about the mountain lions see up there. They left most of the people alone he told everyone. The revival meetings held there drove the mountain lions even higher up the mountain. South on the Ridge was a bluegrass festival playing up a storm and people were having a great time. But the virus had come and it had been quite a while since then. The people on the Ridge had disappeared for the most part to just stay home and the neighborly feeling was gone. The mountain lions were left to run all over, Guy told the boys. This was a sad outcome of the virus. When was things going to get "normal" again, he wondered. The listeners nodded their heads in agreement. There had been a lot of drinking at home up at the Ridge but now people had started to come back down to the town again and there was more awkwardness between neighbors than there used to be. Again, they nodded. It was a time to look forward. Maybe they'd have a good time again. There seemed to be a collective sigh of relief. Whew!

The bookstore reading was a sign of normalcy returning. People were talking about it more as a feature of the change than about the reading itself. It was fine. Robert understood. He just blended in and it was ok to be in the background. It wasn't always like this. Robert had been driven out of places many times in his life. He liked to recount these well-worn tales. His ex-wife told him he was addicted to telling horror stories of his life, especially when he was seeking work. It was like a death wish. Many times, it was the kiss of death to his prospects. His favorite stories that had been published were hard luck ones. When they began to sell, the ex changed her tune but Robert had felt emotionally deserted by then. It was the end of the line. He later wrote more hopeful tales with redemption and self-revival as themes. Kind of where he was now. But he could still fall into the abyss at times. But in the surroundings, he found himself in currently, he didn't think it would happen much. He had already written a piece about performance and the giving of one performer to the ones coming up. It had an optimism that Robert knew he had inside of him but had never expressed in print before.

He rode in his car again. He was going to California to play some gigs. Living the dream at sixty-five. Better late than never. He was reliving the playfulness he had in his childhood, he believed. Then he'd return home for a good long while and keep his performances local.

Was he still in life or had he gone into a permanent dream? He would sometimes get confused with the thought that maybe he was already dead and just looking back or whether he was still alive and driving on the road. For an instant he really didn't know. But when the car started drifting off the road, he knew he was still on Earth. He started thinking how easy it had been in life to just drift buried in the routines of just surviving and not really living. The decisions that one made, the obligations that one had put a person in positions that made it hard to escape. Debts, commitments, occupations and relationships, to name a few. This put one on a path for years, decades or whole lives even. A servitude to the routine, a road of certainty, not the open road to the destination of one's choosing. Whew!

Everything would change. He'd lived long enough to know that.

What a scary thought. A lifetime of deadening routine. Too much to contemplate. But he escaped that death. He was now operating in an open field. Borders, boundaries of only his own making. Nothing to stop him except the scepter of aging, sickness, fate like going off the road. Or another vehicle coming straight at him. Something had happened to Robert. His freedom had finally been realized. He wrote with abandon. He lived without fear. He was on his way forward to unknown destinations. There were people eager to hear his words. He pressed on. He went into a tunnel underneath a mountain. The unknown! What a destination! That was now what it was all about.

He had left behind his entire history. The people who inhabited his stories. The memories that frequented his tales. The dreams he had, consisted of past struggles, problems he had grappled with but never resolved. Dream after dream, he tried to redo these attempts but they still led to emptiness. Tears began to surface. He had become a weepy old-timer. Crying at the drop of a hat. Sentimentally, embarrassingly in public. What was going on, he wondered. How could he stand up to this newly found exploration of life and the imagination? How could he survive intact? All that had been left behind, would it follow his new voyages? It was the material he had been conveying to his new audiences. The following he was seeking, would have to experience this survival of the past struggles. He needed to present a strong façade, not a weepy old fool who yearned to get under the covers. Who wanted to hide in his new house, so hard-fought to land in. Those faces searching for a laugh, a sense that all turns out all right. That there was some kind of promise, treasure at the end of one's rainbow. Not a quivering bowl of Jello awash in self-doubt. Whew! He almost crashed again. This was getting ridiculous. He would have to look for a place to stop for the night. Coming up on Little Rock,

Arkansas. About fifty years ago, he stopped there. He woke up in the morning with all his belongings either gone or strewn around the parking lot. Like when he had lived in that terrible part of New York City advertised as a loft, when those were new but the place was ghetto-like and people slept on his car's roof and he witnessed neighbors throw their garbage out the window. Every day, first thing in the morning. He had left his life for an impossible dream. How many times had he done that? Too many. Never to really learn his lesson. But he would escape those scrapes, bruises, scratches, the knocks life throws at one's head. No matter how many times you duck. It connects quite a bit and you hit the canvas. You are ok if you get up. The if is what is the deciding factor. He remembers the story of having his life portrayed on the stage and the feeling of so much vulnerability afterwards that he stopped speaking publicly for two years. Hiding in the city. Hiding from family. From all the friends he had made. Growing mutely insane. Walking a tightrope until almost falling off. Having an internal battle going on inside like no other ever burned inside of him. Thinking he was going to step off every ledge he walked nearby. Thinking his self-loathing would prevail and his mind would simply fold up on itself. Like a bitter toxin. He finally dodged this threat by completely embarrassing himself in a plea for help. Thus, he began to speak again. More and more. Incessantly for quite some time. He had met the enemy inside of himself and it almost vanquished him. But then he went on. Robert got to a motel and retired for the night.

Breakfast was incredible! People were emerging after the enforced hiatus of the virus. Everyone was hungry for many things. Food, companionship, gossip, news, and community. A lady got up from her table and began to sing "The Green, Green Grass of Home". A man hugged everyone in the dining room as he exited. Tears dampened in his eyes. The birds were singing and relief was in the air. The sun was shining. Robert felt this was a great sign to make his way to Texas. He called some people back home in the Northeast. Everyone was fine. But they were still under the orders to stay home. We never had orders like that in our lives. Yet so many fell under the lash. They got used to it so quickly. Like it was a usual thing. The specter of the unknown, surmised Robert. The unknown was extremely powerful. He was approaching the ultimate unknown. He lived, he loved, he created, he shared with others. He had no regrets. He had nothing to fear, he guessed. He hit a pothole and was again reminded to pay attention to the road. He loved the road and yearned to be on it for many years. He was ready to stay on it though he also yearned to be back in his beloved home in the beautiful mountains Hopefully, by the grace of God he would return one day. He thought of Margery. Years before, too many to recall, she was a soulmate who turned into a cellmate, figuratively. Neither could negotiate life at the time. Stumbling in the dark for a short period of time. It went bad fast and they ran out of gas. Too much crashing into walls. When she fell upon him and tried to crush his windpipe, it was time to call it quits. A lot of drugging and drinking did not help. She left him penniless on a corner with no place to go, yet grateful to be going. He could only go up from there. Young people do not know much. Whew! Just thinking about his frame of mind at that time, gave Robert great pause. He pulled over to compose himself. Then on with the ride.

The next thing that came into Robert's mind was this summer romance of many years ago. He had driven his girl home after living and working away from their homes. She lived in another city. Robert had been fighting his feelings all the way on that ride. There was a foreboding sadness of endings permeating the car. That whatever had transpired in the bucolic summer setting was disappearing. No words were said. It floated on the crisp air. Robert was trying to keep the romance alive for the coming year but she had shown no inclination. Robert drove by a relative's house, "save me from this," he silently pleaded. It was surreal. Robert brought up a couple of great experiences they had shared. They reached Lydia's house. Her family was excited to have her home. Robert felt like an odd man out. Everyone was nice and so polite. They had a nice meal and it was time to go. Robert stumbled explaining his plan for the winter of sharing time together. Lydia only stared at the ground. As Robert said goodbye, he opened the car door and a bee immediately stung his ankle. As the painful twilight descended, he knew it was over.

As Robert progressed to Texas, he received word that he would be reading from his new book in Dallas in two days. He always liked Dallas. Everything was big there and people there did big things. He got both excited and nervous at the same time. All of this reading in public was new to him. Writing books, being invited to places, all new. It was a beyond his wildest dreams thing to Robert. He noticed he was speeding. A cop flew by. Whew! Close!

Thoughts now came fast. His parents love, yet their disapproval. His lack of helpfulness to his siblings, yet paid back later in life at critical times. Feelings of worthlessness as a father, yet his devotion proven many times, yet the little expectations his children had from him. His heart broke at the selfishness those in his life felt he showed. Yet, yet, yet… Life comes and goes, quick and slow. Feelings both high and low. Depending on the season. Offering all the reasons and on and on. The playgrounds of his youth. The daily feelings of realizations, sounds, smells, colors, hurts and defeats in the games. Victories and pride in the play of the moment. All the twilights as days end. So much promise in the days to come of which they seem never-ending. The running, jumping, laughing and hollering, changing into the seriousness of adulthood. Who would take that trade in retrospect? Creativity was Robert's only response. Up onto this day. This day he streaks across the wide expanse of Texas. Feeling like a speck of dust but his mind teeming with gusts of insight. Rushing towards the best days of his life. Hoping they would be slow to end. Hoping his physical being would support his spiritual being. At least for a while longer. Rushing through the night to get to the destination where he could meet people. People who wanted to meet him with nothing but the past behind him. Whew!

It was almost too much to contemplate.

PAJAMAS

*S*oon we'll be in pajamas. The three of us. Enveloped in them. Safe, warm and comfortable. They keep us happy especially if they have turquoise prints like fake tattoos on a white background. What a marvelous invention! All blows are cushioned absolutely cushioned if they have padded feet. Rubber feet. Rubber pads, that is. They cure Daddy's stress. They decompress Mommy's blues. They tell me my school day has ended and I'm close to laying my head on my pillow. I like pillows too. It means all troubles are gone until another day starts. It's time to rest and we are all blessed. Simple. At least for now. Nobody's bugging me, not in my class or in my extracurriculars or on the street on the way home or on the way to school. 'cause even though I'm a kid there's plenty of strife in my life. I'm sure Daddy and Mommy love their pajamas, too. Though they may stall their time in them by staying up late. They'll have to get to the moment of putting on their pajamas, too. Pajamas are the most...they are so important to hold onto for however long you can. For everybody is in the same big boat and we all need our blows cushioned and those fake tattoos with the mottos and little sayings in turquoise will keep us ok for at least another day.

IT'S ALL IN THE JEANS!

*B*efore I undertake anything creative, I line up all of my blue jeans of which I have too many. I put them all around whatever room I'm working in. I put them in three piles. Best, pretty good and alright. Done this for at least three and a half decades. Jeans mean much to me and the more perfectly faded, the more they mean. If they are really my best ones, I have trouble wearing them. I'd rather admire them. But I digress, I think…This embarrassment of riches all comes from deprivation. My mother never bought me real ones. They were those fake jeans they used to sell (and probably still do) in the discount stores. I pined for just one real pair but only when I was grown and became my own benefactor could I load up on them and load up I have, I must say. My child would look at me oddly. Then my cats would eye me suspiciously until I left the room and then they would destroy the piles and bask in their destruction. My wife crowned me with mass looks of eternal disapproval. Who can blame her? But it fuels my courage to embark on a new frightening creative project. You need encouragement to face a blank slate. And I get mine from the jeans. Laugh if you want. I'm used to the scorn. I will always do it until the end. I'm sure of this. Three sure things. Death, taxes and jeans. Inevitable! They can't let me down like people.

FOR MEN, FUNNY IS EVERYTHING #2

I speak for myself, ladies, but I believe most men care most about being funny, especially in front of women. And sometimes children, too. Do you know this? Probably. Do children know this? Well, in my case, when my daughter was very young, she would hurt me by saying ,"not funny, not funny" when I tried to cajole her out of sadness. It hurt at least as much as her sadness if truth be told. If I was a comedian and I bombed onstage, a silent audience couldn't hurt me more. If I don't have a joke in a new social situation, I have nothing to say. If I'm speaking to a group, I better have a funny opening and more importantly, I must get laughs. If not, I am done for. A plodding drone will emerge or worse, an in the ozone kind of quality will imbue my speech. I'll be speaking to myself. It will feel that way. If someone tells me, "you are performing a service, you are not performing, it's a good thing". Well, I say, who cares? No laughs, it's like suicide. Maybe it's just me. Perhaps I'm a silly man. But everywhere I see men trying out lines. They could be pick up lines, getting a job lines. They could be hosting lines, welcoming lines, quantifying, stupefying, mystifying, crucifying lines but they are all in search of a laugh. A true beacon of light moment in their trying universe. All of the effort, sweat, might, seeking, bending, searching, lurching and all the hope on the line just for a meager laugh. A kindly, gut bucket one. A guffaw, grimace, eye-rolling, gasping, coughing one or even a desperate, anything as long as it is a goddamn bursting, full of humor and joy, happy laugh. It means the world to me, um, us, I truly believe with all my heart. We need it, take it from me. We just want to return home. Lie in our beds with our spirits soaring. Our chests brimming with pride and our souls filled with fulfillment, happy as hell. We got our laugh, or approval, pat on the head, look of admiration. Like the little boy I am, we are. Like our first win, our first look of approval that we received from our mothers. Our fathers, doesn't mean the same, does it? I'm just guessing but maybe it goes all the way back to our most impressionable times. We never really lose it.

So next time you see a man reaching deep for a laugh to make a first impression, remember that this may be a reincarnation of many important moments of his life scattered in his subconscious. Buried so deep in his essence that he may not survive the next indifference to his wit, his delivery, his material of comic invention that lays awaiting to be sprung on his next innocent encounter.

A man might have boatloads of money. Earned much respect. Received mucho affection. Achieved tremendous prestige. Possesses a great pedigree. Rides a truckful of momentum. Holds a wealth of honor. Wields a mountain of power. Beholds a crowd of admirers. But he stands incomplete without laughs at his own sense of humor, especially from ladies. To be funny for a man means everything!

WIND CHIMES

*T*hough I'm six million miles away from Earth sitting in my space cruiser I can hear echoes of wind chimes from earliest memories. Wind is my personal guide from way back. It has taught me to forge my life and my goals on its wings. I became a pilot before I became a mother and then I went further into space travel. No one could stop me. I had to listen to a lot of male ego points and false directives that tried to keep me in place. When I reached a certain plateau to call some shots I went back into it again, a new ladder to climb to get on this mission. Now that I am here, I've got a few things to say to the world. I need to address my husband, Chuck too.

Now that everything is dark and quiet. Now, maybe, I can finally express myself. To myself. I like the dark. Nothing is exposed. I'm not threatened by the dark, Chuck. I need to say a few things, just a few. About a little girl in a green nightdress in the night on a farm in the West with her hands over her ears because of the noise from her house crashing into the stillness and silence of the open land outside. You're not the only one with feelings, Chuck. And about the woman who wants so much to be living her dream of who she wants to be and how nothing comes easy and you're pulled in one direction and then get reversed by the distraction of mere survival. Disappointment, frustration, deep swallow, hold breath. Having freedom of choice and yet none at all. Fed up, yet just getting ready to begin. Skipping, turning, twisting in one spot and poised to move to another. Waiting, wailing. Getting to the dream or lurching back to the same nowhere quicksand. CHUCK, you run into walls with such fury while I twist and cringe in my own river and SCREAM and

deep down, real deep down, still see, still feel...the girl on the farm in
the green nightdress, whipping in the wind in the dark. Swallowed up
by others. And dreaming of only HERSELF.

PURPLE FRINGE

He wore a purple fringe jacket which announced his arrival with just enough fanfare. I was new to the neighborhood and he befriended me. He lived over the railroad tracks. My older friends did not like him. His brother was a bookie. His father was a gangster. I never knew Jews like that. He wore a purple fringe jacket and he sold the drugs in the neighborhood. A lot of people didn't like him. He told tall tales. People didn't believe them. He was a bad influence they told me. He was someone who welcomed me with open arms when I was the new kid in the neighborhood. I met people through him. He was outlandish in his cowboy suede purple fringe jacket. Like he could cover up his deficiencies with all that color and flair. The illegal activity, the crooked way of doing things. I thought he was fun. My friends thought he was trouble. I thought he was funny. They thought he was sad. I didn't get it. Not too many could boss me around but he could. We stayed up all night on uppers talking. I felt like I was going straight up to heaven that night. But we were planning something stupid.

I was told he got killed a few years later. A deal gone bad. My friends stayed away from him. I didn't until I had to. He got out of control, sort of. But I used to think he was funny, my friends said he was sad. His brother was a bookie. He lived over the railroad tracks. His father was a gangster. His mother had a hole in her throat from smoking. She had to cover it when she talked. She was very nice. Her diet pills made us feel like we were going straight up to heaven when we popped them. He died a drug dealer's death. The family were risk-takers. I didn't know any other Jews like them. Purple fringe gives me a twinge when I remember him.

MEMORIES SO MIXED UP
MIGHT AS WELL MAKE THEM UP

*B*oris Karpowitz grew up in Brooklyn in the 1960's. Certain memories have stuck in his mind. When asked if he believes in God, he always recounts this story.

"I was in this special high school in New York City. You had to take a test to get into this school. I was always smart in school. My mother wanted me to go there. I took the entrance test. I had a very high fever that morning. I must have scored very high because I wound up with the kids who were assigned 2 science classes in their first year and more the next. I was not good anymore in Math and Science by the 10th grade. Everyone in this school seemed way smarter than me. They were like computers. I never felt so inferior until I went to that school. I became a class cutter and student protester. I smoked pot and roamed the City during school hours. I was failing Chemistry and our teacher Mr. Andromides gave us a test with a bonus question worth as much as the rest of the test if we got it right. Well, I drew a blank on most of the test. When I got to the bonus, I asked God to provide me with the answer. I sweated bullets as I waited. My mother's disappointed face appeared in my mind's eye. Suddenly, the number 34 popped into my mind and I wrote it on the paper. The next day, Mr. Andromides announced that only one student had gotten the bonus question right. Boris Karpowitz, come up and get your grade. 89. Next class, Karpowitz plan to instruct the class on how you solved the problem. Shit, I added it up wrong someone muttered behind me. It was Paul Zim, the best student in the class. I grabbed him after class and we went through the problem together. I memorized Zim's process and I retold it to the class as if it was mine. I added the numbers up correctly to total 34. I have believed in God ever since."

Gene Blizzo was hired by the New York City Department of Social Services. He was assigned to the local office that covered his childhood neighborhood in Queens, New York. He arrived with another trainee. The supervisor gave her a caseload but there was none for Gene. "We'll send you out on cases that need extra care", said the supe. First Gene went with Jacques, a worker approaching retirement age. "Never rob the clients of their problems for it is all they have", was a favorite Jacques-ism. They went to a Mrs. Loquiam who was unable to manage her finances or shopping any longer. "We are going to the center of the solar system (her bank) ", he told her. "We will take my space cruiser" as we entered Jacques's car. "Let's see the man from Uncle Sam (the bank teller). Let's make out a check and move on to our next mission". And so, it went. Supe then had me question a short man who lived alone who complained he had been constantly robbed and beaten. I interviewed Hans. "They made me buy them all drinks and then they clubbed me", he said. Found locked out of his apartment and penniless, he was in his hallway. Gene got him squared away and left Hans in his apartment by the end of the workday. The next morning there was a new complaint from Hans' neighbor. Hans was found in the street bleeding and penniless. Gene went to get him out of the precinct and took him home. "What happened, Hans?" "I went out and a little old man followed me to the bar. He took my wallet and ordered drinks for everybody. He hit me over the head and these boys took the rest of my money, my shoes and dropped me on the curb right in front of my building". Gene talked to the supe who told him to straighten Hans out again and work the night and keep a surveillance on Hans. Later that night, Hans left his apartment and went to the bar. He closed the place down and staggered to his building. He fell on the ground on his corner and was unconscious. Gene roused Hans. "Well, did you see the old guy?" Hans asked.

Gene was now ready for his own special cases. Jacques soon retired and Gene inherited his people.

Rod Dentifriss had been a drug addict. He lost his friends, family, jobs, career, memory most of his mind and ambition. Then he got clean and regained most of those things back. He was celebrating his second anniversary in a twelve-step program at his home meeting. People liked him and they came from meetings all around. One lady was a belly dancer from Rio de Janeiro and another was a jazz musician. Rod had several of his records. One person knew Rod best. Keno Wallace. Keno spoke for Rod. He said, "Two years ago, I met Rod. He was unemployable and now he's leading a union revolt." This was true. Rod had kept nearly 100 people where he worked out of their work space for 2 months because trucks were idling outside the doors, pouring their exhausts into the office. "He was a scared guy, apologizing for his existence and now he's seen with an exotic dancer at his side, the envy of all his friends", Keno went on. This was a little bit true but only in that Rod helped the dancer get bookings through some networking. "He's been seen parading around the nightclubs with his jazz friends and I believe he is writing an Off Broadway show about musicians", Keno kept on. Really, it was a pipe dream at this point, a very poor man's version of a life story with some taped jazz behind the acting. "And now let's hear it for our celebrant, Rod D", thunderous applause. If I remember it correctly.

There was this time Bobby Josephson took a train to New Haven and ran into his alter ego idol, Isaac. He was a very successful director who was going up to Yale to pick the directing applicants for the Graduate School of which four or five were picked out of a thousand. It happened right after Bobby had tried to meet Isaac to share his frustrating path in the same profession. The man had no time and bam! Bobby winds up taking the same train and riding with him for a couple of hours. The parallels in their careers were so similar yet the results so vastly different. Both integrated music constantly in the plays they chose to direct. Even the choice of plays was identical at times. The genres they chose also were similar from German post-war realism to cowboy rock. From jazz scores to European music. Both men were Hungarian. Isaac had dropped out of high school and hit it big in the big city. Bobby paid a lot of school and internship dues but terrible coincidences had doomed many a hopeful beginning. Deaths ending breakthrough proposed productions, for example. Third and final interviews to run theaters resulted in blind alleys. A death occurring the night before a meeting to get crucial advice to possibly front a group to take over a famous theater and so on. A wincing Isaac told Bobby that their paths were strikingly and creatively similar but the timing differences were equally contrasting. He encouraged the hard luck Bobby to keep going and maybe his luck would change. Well, over the years some good things did happen for Bobby but prosperity nor public acclaim never materialized. Their work remained so similar that they were mistaken for each other at times. The most interesting element of their meeting on the train was that the high school dropout was going to pick the cream of the crop at the most prestigious drama school in America while the other was still chasing the beginnings of a career after many years. Isaac bade a hasty retreat. He did not want to catch the others' reality. Not for an instant. Bobby could not blame him.

Many years later Bobby found out that his role model had died. In Isaac's bio it stated that he was a college graduate. So much for the high school dropout story. He had originally wanted to be a writer but switched to directing plays. It dawned on Bobby that Isaac had made it a better story, a dropout choosing the uber competitive students. Bobby had written and had produced some plays. He also had written and published stories. Bobby had felt some success by then. He felt that at least Isaac's recognition as a director represented the work, they both had arrived at on their own. He had forged his own path and could feel good about himself, too.

"We have to make the most of what life we have left", she said, looking right at me. It went through me like a knife. Both of us in our sixties we met by happenstance. It became a lifechanging moment for me. It permeated my consciousness and made me accountable for every moment since. It has made me jump into so many situations I never processed that it sped my life up until it went too fast for me. I was an old sixty plus. I had been slowing down for years. I now had trouble getting out of bed in the mornings now that I had no job to go to. My mind went on long tripping rides at night listening to my favorite songs. I went on long writing jaunts during the day and saw the most beautiful scenery riding around where I lived. But I had trouble with that notion she had told me that rocked my world. Was I doing the most, making the most? Truly? It kept haunting me. I was treated to so much love by my loved ones. Had new and great friendships by new and old friends. But I still felt behind. I was chasing a life fleeting. Discovering but not fully tasting. Slowing down, crying out with loss after finally realizing comfort and self-fulfillment. I was just coming into my life. There was peace and serenity I had sought all my life. Yet now I was chasing a bucking bronco with a last gasp of life on a gallop. I sat down and finally saw what I needed to see! What a lucky so and so I was. And wasn't that enough?

No, it wasn't! There was no rule for this. There was no answer. What I felt was all that mattered. This was why people held onto life, never wanting to die, unless they were in relentless, excruciating pain. But this feeling of not fully living every day was also painful. Could I run again? Well, I could move a little. Could I chase dreams down again? No thanks, too many lifetimes of that already. I welcomed the giving up of that. It accounted for the peace I had just newly achieved. My whole being wanted this full life again but it crashed against what I had built and my reluctance to now embrace it. Oh, this was getting too existential! My inner being cried, "Stop! You can't go against me anymore." You have what you want and what you need. Just relax. Life is to be enjoyed and not continually yearned for. Don't you finally get it? Act your age and go quietly into the night.

If Charlie Sylvester had not told me this tale himself, I would not have believed it. It is not politically correct. It took courage to live it and it takes some to tell it. Charlie was a theater director making a comeback in his career as well as in his life. As he committed to straightening out his life, he also got his first directing job in years. He was still shaky but he accepted it. It was a play about a jazz man. He didn't know anything about the subject but he studied up quickly and got a good grasp of the character and his music. It was a one man show. He scouted an actor, B, who was appearing in a hit Off Broadway show. Charlie thought he could hire B as the show was to close soon. The producer, L, was also the playwright and Charlie had a history with him. Charlie had given L research about these other musicians and as Charlie had not been a writer as yet, he thought L could write the play. L had in the meantime written a play about these musicians and told Charlie that once the current play was up, he'd show Charlie what he'd written on the other project. L, as the producer and playwright, didn't believe Charlie could get the actor Charlie had scouted but Charlie did get him for the show. Charlie and B had a great connection and Charlie fashioned a score of the subject's music to go along with the acting of this one man show. L had written another shorter play to go along with the show Charlie was directing. It was a very militant piece about a Jewish mayor and his treatment of the black people in New York City at the time. Charlie did not know anything about the companion piece until dress rehearsal when he was outraged by what he saw as a Jewish person. Both horrified by the Anti Semitism and reverse racism in the play, Charlie could not stomach not warning the people who came to see his show about the musician about the other play. This caused a problem with L, naturally.

Meanwhile, there was no stage manager hired until the dress rehearsal. There were numerous sound cues that needed much prior rehearsal to get familiar with the sound to be run. The stage manager merely turned off the whole score to listen to the actor and when Charlie ran in to straighten things out. He was beaten and called a Jew like L's other play stated. No one stood up for Charlie and he felt in danger with the cast and staff. Yet he was so proud of his directing work, so he had to be accompanied by bodyguards to attend his show. L did not back him up and did not show him the play which Charlie had given him both the idea and research.

A few months later, L called Charlie and let him know that his direction was up for the Black Theater Awards. The winners were not yet announced but if Charlie was to win, L would let him know so he could attend and show the people who they gave the award to. He didn't win but the point was made by L.

Years later, L did show Charlie the play. Charlie didn't think it was good enough. Charlie wrote his own version around the original story. For years both versions circulated around New York, L's version was picked up first and later Charlie's was finally chosen for a more prestigious run. It took many years. Charlie has been thinking of turning this story into a play one day. The theme would be: A Director Can Only Attend His Show Accompanied by Bodyguards!

HAVE YOU MET THE COOKIE MAN?

(FOR JO JACOBSON)

We were all down and out with no options left except jails, institutions and death. We'd gotten the message together in various forms of certainty. We found ourselves in a burned out building that held meetings. Faces and bodies were in half light, like silhouettes. Chairs mighty hard. The coffee was brutal and you could barely make out the corners of the rooms but you would see outlines of bodies in various states of sleep, comas or maybe even death. This crowd was rough. Any whiff of self-pity was met with a terse, "Here's a five or a ten, take it and go out and die!" "Don't want to hear any whining!" Tough crowd like I said. We were like zombies trying to pick up our pace. Some had hours, days a few had weeks away from the stuff that had laid us low and almost killed us. There were stars among us but mainly we were losers at life. My best buddy and I were refugees from the theater. I had trouble getting started and my friend was shot. We travelled from one meeting to the next on our last legs. Dead financially, our spirits careening and chafed raw in all directions. Plenty of time to kill our energy flagging, at times, prodigious at others and then half asleep. We sang songs of Broadway through the streets. Songs of hope, happiness and victory. Strangers joined in the celebration as we got another hour, another five blocks under our belts. Like flowers stretching toward the sun, we belted out music from The Fantasticks, Anything Goes, West Side Story, Fiddler! People would call out "Look it's the Cookie Man!" My friend resembled someone on TV and on billboards pitching a new line of cookies. It was all so humorous, fun in our unfocused and frenzied march through the busiest city in the world. Sooner or later someone more stable would stake us to a burger or a coffee or maybe a job lead. And hope would fuel us through more time. We would laugh uproariously-ly-maybe life would let us back in? My buddy with his knuckles red and white, wrists with permanent scars. I was wearing pants from my earliest teen years now at the age of twenty-nine fitting again. This guy, Bill talking in numbers and streets. Dickie living in a closet in a men's shelter fighting for one day sober. Unable to go back to Minnesota because the law and his in laws were after him. Bridges burned and each step for all of us uncertain. Also, Ken who lived in a fancy building in the West Village but was heading downhill with a fortune buried somewhere he forgot and couldn't stay straight. Heroin always on the corner and people waiting for the end. It took almost a year but the end did come for him. Tragic but not unexpected. Up and down, side to side, we combed the streets killing time and amusing those around us as time passed so slow. The promise of freedom buoyed us. "Yeah, he is the Cookie Man", we would announce, "step right up and we'll entertain you, Seventy-six Trombones…" Reality could actually be fun we would tell each other. For some it became so and they got a new life. For Dickie and Ken it didn't happen. The odds were never good for most of us. A very harsh territory to resurrect in. But for the Cookie Man and I, we made it through. And we stay grateful and don't take much for granted these days.

THE POET OF COMEDY

Rudyard was a performing poet. He liked to use language in ways that simultaneously astounded and entertained his audiences. Mainly he amazed them. He drew audiences like crazy in a place where it was difficult to draw large audiences. Rudyard transposed scary poetic classics or spiritual or political probes into accessible trifles. Masterpieces into pop idioms. Dramatics both timeless and semantically melodious into Hallmark dramas with salacious twists. But more than anything he was silly. He took his poetry seriously and loved employing a million-dollar vocabulary to create a thin veneer of sloganeering or upon a trove of slapstick comedy. He just loved the sound of laughter too much and couldn't resist hearing it. He loved the feel of full houses and it was like pulling the wool over the public's eyes that a true poet could pull this off. He employed a musical partner, Felix, who was a veteran of the Sixties' Folk scene. The pair presented little playlets, cartoon-like political motifs and re-imagined poems to the delight of thousands. No matter how many times people saw the duo they always retained the sense of adventure in their performances. And always they were silly. Rudyard and Felix were true champions for other performers. They treated their peers, as if they too were as popular and gifted as the two of them were. Rudyard had press credentials as well. He had been a major editor of arts journals and ghosted many articles previewing other shows and acts with a generosity quite rare in the culture. This made him very beloved by his contemporaries. Now, he had no patience for critics who used their pulpit to aggrandize their own importance. A particular reviewer put her own comfort such as heat or lack thereof a theater space over whether to print a review or feature on an artist. When once slighted by her imperious whims to wield her own comfort over the efforts of my theater group, I received this note from Rudyard. "Many times, I would peer out into the house and encountered her unsmiling visage. While possessing no discerning taste cut with her chief characteristic of chronic dissatisfaction, she has mainly distinguished herself to cast seeds of ignorance upon many a talented subject. A smidgeon of humility would greatly benefit her, but alas she merely grows older with time. Ignore her dismissal of your valiant effort and your audience will find you in time".

And with these kind words I was the recipient of the charitable kinship of a fellow artist. I was given freely this act of kindness mixed with poetic justice that the situation deserved. Presented by one who instinctively knew that poetry and comedy could be inextricably linked through performance. Joy transmitted to the many who witnessed Rudyard perform true magic.

THE LIFERS

*T*here was a lifer. She spent her life as art. Everything she touched was an expression of how she felt. She created. Everywhere she went was photographed with an expression, that is, an impression, hers, of it. A point of view. She identified with these impressions. They were her day, her relationship to them, where they fit in this retrospective of her life constantly on display. She was doing it at age seven and still doing it today. She has been a wife, a mother, a teacher a friend, a sister, a daughter. If I was a writer, she'd be a subject of mine in a book. She is both a life force and a lifer in creativity. One has to admire her commitment and her prolific output. She gives it, practices it and passes it on. That's the lifer's way. I say, brilliant, she says maybe. I say that's exemplary, she responds, to you, I guess. I say, keep going, she asks, do I have a choice, I think not.

There was a man who lost his child. He remained grief-stricken for the rest of his life. He stopped practicing what he was trained for, the law. He gave lessons to those who wanted to change their lives and needed a structure. He was first seen as a charlatan, as most who offer something for nothing usually are. But he did it for his own survival. To ward off the grief that was eating at him. To fill the void that death had planted. Many were helped which gave this man another day to survive on this Earth. He was a Lifer of delivering a path of redemption. A way to go on living for the ones who had to change. The only price was willingness on the part of the students. The teacher was there for them for life.

I knew another Lifer. She was a zaftig woman with a great heart and mind. She overcame a painful personal loss by helping the needy every day. She treated people with dignity and compassion no matter what sickness or ill feeling they might express to the world. She gives plenty of herself to her family and still believes in the good of people throughout all the trials and tribulations that selfishness and politics proliferate throughout the community. Still lives in the house she grew up in and when life gets her down, she gives more to get out of it. The world gives her much less than she gives it. It takes a Lifer to do that.

Another Lifer is an immigrant woman I came across. Principled and tough with an incredible work ethic that beats the band. A beautiful smile and beacon to her children as she survived who knows what where she came from in Africa. She survived a horrific auto accident in America which makes it painful to still come to work. Administrators attempting to cut down her pride and chasten her strength but you can't keep righteousness down especially when the commitment is so powerful to do good and to do God's work for others. These are just a few examples of great people I have met and knew. I am richer for it and will always value their friendship.

A FRIENDLY DYBBUK

*I*t had been a little over a year since Robby's father had passed. He was on the last leg of the show's tour. The show was an open tribute to his father. Robby's father, Samuel, was what you would call a common, working man. Humble, perhaps to a fault. Honest, never used shortcuts. Devoted, to his family, work and most importantly to his religion. More so, as he aged.

Robby had many quarrels and more resentments with his old man. But upon writing the tribute, he became in touch with a deep love that resulted in tears quite frequently. So much had not been expressed between them. The only demonstrated reveal was that his father always wanted Robby to return to the family home. Samuel got that wish, in his last two years as Robby commuted to his job too far away from his home to return every day. Therefore, Robby did stay at his Dad's house several days a week.

Samuel shared his pain with his son. He was obsessed with the wish to die and actively searched for the final disease that would take him. He finally found it. A little over a year ago.

The previous performance had taken place in a very comfortable space. Robby did not like his performance that night. He felt outside the text, watching himself perform. It confirmed why he was not a performer but a director, a writer. Always, until this show. This was special and his to deliver. It was a loving and fulfilling endeavor, usually. The place Robby was performing this night was an Orthodox synagogue. A classroom with fluorescent lights. The audience all around, inches away and packed to the gills. Quite a daunting task for one who lacked confidence and recovering from such a self-conscious effort.

Robby concentrated as if his life depended on it. He was so focused Samuel appeared and infiltrated his entire being throughout the whole show. Like a friendly dybbuk. It was as if being transported to Heaven and dropped at the curtain call.

THE BYSTANDER

Chapter One
LOST CAUSE

There were no chestnuts in the supermarkets that year. Ben Levis did not remember any other winter in many years that there were no chestnuts. Odd. There were many other things missing that year but chestnuts are what he especially noticed. Things had been feeling smaller. The holidays. He was like a spectator not a participant. Barely Thanksgiving and they were over as far as he was concerned. The relatives had dwindled. Not that he was ever comfortable when there were more relatives. But now it was non-existent. A non-existent family. He watched the rest of America go through it. He had no more obligations. They had been taken away from him. Behavior and accusations had done the job.

The last event where he had been accused of robbing relatives exiled him permanently. Being innocent of a crime and getting tagged by "loved ones" was a real eye-opener. One that he wouldn't recommend nor even discuss with others. Thank God he had one confidant who had been an attorney and Ben was given guidance. Had that not been the case, he'd be even more lost. What he had learned was that he did not have the meanness to be able to even conceive of what he was accused of. He also was not capable to carry out that kind of deceit on another human being let alone a relative that had given so much to Ben as he grew up. Just going over this in his mind made him shake with anger. Made him want to do vengeance. Made him so estranged from all in his family who even entertained this thought that he might have done such a deed… better to just go his own way. And so, he did. He continued to be the human being he always was. He helped many people in his work as a social service provider. He continued his creative work as a theater maker. He cut off those that either did him evil or those that believed those that linked him with evil. He had a chestnut and relative-free holiday season and felt better for it than before he received his confidant's advice.

Now the behavior referred to in the previous part of the story was Ben's instability emotionally. He could not be counted on in simple ways. This defect caused much uncertainty and pain for others. He always seemed about ten or twenty years behind in his feelings compared to his actions. Getting married had a delayed effect on him. Becoming a father left him somewhat paralyzed. He was something of a missing link both as a husband and as a father. He put more thoughtfulness and focus in other areas which defied the nature of his commitments that he had made. He was left on the outside looking in. A place that drove him kind of crazy and he went into estrangement mode. This was a dangerous intersection in his life. Though it left him feeling empty and hollow being alone was not his destiny. He still was a father and husband. It would be many years until he became an ex-husband.

That bridge was one he had much trepidation to cross. He had taken baby steps towards it but never followed through. Many years he dwelled in an emotional tunnel trapped in a muffled scream. His bizarre behavior of being simultaneously a role model family man and a ghost to those who knew better was never reconciled. His outer coldness belied a buried warmth. He threw himself into pursuits far away from the rewards of close family life. His instincts were thwarted so frequently, he could not feel their presence. Long under the influence of drugs and alcohol, he lived sober many more years yet this inner struggle remained unresolved. Twists and turns only confused him more and more. Living an examined life only served his ambivalence and further entangled him in his own web. Thus, he emerged on his own. An older man on the precipice of many options yet with no apparent direction. He was wondering where his waning years would take him.

Images of past family life overwhelmed his dreams.

The birth of his baby girl. He laughed and cried at the same time.

His proposal to his wife in the middle of Times Square.

His overpowering hunger as a ten-year-old eating ten pieces of toast after a trip from New York City to Washington D.C. with his beloved Aunt Betty.

His daughter playing a song from Ben's show on the violin as part of her Bat Mitzvah.

His father giving advice to his friends at the bungalow colony in the Catskills as if he was a sage.

His father running out of the casino at the same colony on "Strippers' Night".

His mother so strange, she was so popular with her friends.

His mother criticizing his father, Ben and his wife.

His brother entertaining all the relatives at Ben's Bar Mitzvah with songs and jokes. His brother was only four years old.

His parents liked his brother better.

His wife so mad when Ben left her. But it showed how much she loved him.

His cousin from Hungary was like a sister at one time. She told him to open his eyes and see how his wife loved him.

Ben returned to his family that time.

He struggled up Yosemite like a coward and came down from the top like a victorious warrior.

Yelling "oh, jive!" jumping into a pool as his daughter howled with laughter.

Riding bikes with his daughter on a blistering hot day saying, "Feel the coolness!"

His grandmother so disappointed in Ben for disrespecting his mother when he was a teenager.

His father searching his dresser and finding drugs.

His mother catching him returning home on an acid trip.

Staying up all night on said acid trip and watching cartoons play on his bedroom walls.

Leaving his wife for the last time.

Hearing his daughter say "you never should have come back when I was a kid".

Being accused by his cousins of stealing his Aunt Betty's money.

Only the last thing didn't happen and wasn't really in any of Ben's dreams.

But the accusation did happen.

Ben discovered something in time. You could only be yourself. A version not of one's own making or someone else's version but only of the true version of himself. That was who he was and it cost a total separation from family in Ben's case. It occurred over many years but he found himself on a road he never imagined he would travel. He had to be on his own, no matter how hard it would be. He got out of his life and wound up very far away from the life he had known. He lived in a little cabin with only a little water stream and in the shadow of a great mountain with very little man made stimuli in his environment. Most of his life had ebbed with his youth and he was to face himself and dwell in the shadows life had wrought. There would be no more rules or obligations for Ben Levis. The world he had left began to rage and boil in its toxicity. He had become an alien with only a small town as civilization and stream to waterfall to mountain to cliff the neighborhood of his whole world. The past was slowly becoming a whirlpool of memory slipping off into a distant reality unrecognizable to his consciousness. The alienated human who was once Ben Levis became the hermit known as Boris Musikrant of the town Silas in the state of South Carolina. His mail and phone messages were collected in the little town and picked up once a month by the recipient. Ben, now known as Boris was free as a bird with perhaps less roots. He was free to think, sleep, ruminate and create upon his soul's desires. He was developing a new way of producing thoughts and ideas and could only test them out on himself and sometimes whatever critter chose to stop by the cabin.

Now up in the Northeast where Ben had lived warfare kind of broke out between those that wanted to break society and those who wanted to preserve it. The breakers were in the majority and there was a panic all over where people lived. The notion that the world might end was fast becoming a deeply held belief. Those that could remain blind to this were profoundly gifted. Life could be a lost cause was not a fallacy anymore and had begun to be people's reality no matter what side they were situated. Ben, now Boris experienced only a wisp of this as he could only read about it on the Internet when he so chose to look in on this world he had departed from physically.

Boris kept up with one person from his past. Her name was Ann and she was a person he trusted more than anyone. She tried to keep him apprised but her work was so encompassing as a community leader that their connection was sporadic. When the Levis world crumbled, Ann had been a witness to it. He had taken her into his confidence and when he departed, only Ann knew his whereabouts and his new name. When Ben needed information to prove his family's accusations were phony, Ann helped him uncover it. She knew everything and knew always where he was coming from. She also knew where and why he had begun a new identity and location. Though she helped many a lost cause she knew Boris Musikrant was not one.

The rest of the story will now shift from a narrator's voice to the voice of Boris Musikrant.

Chapter Two
DREAM SLEEP

I swear I have been in a dream sleep. Been in one my whole life. Don't really know if I'm living this life or merely dreaming it. I look back ten, twenty years and I can't believe that person did the things he did. Ever happen to you? Like it was somebody else. A different energy, courage, a mind that knew no fear. He does not have much relation to the person I am today. I get brought up short to all of that. Who was that? Then again, who was that? Which leads me to the belief that I have already lived multiple lifetimes. When younger, I just lived. You have to be older to feel these things. To believe these things. Strange, mystifying. Makes me feel I have lived a few lives. The old guy in today's mirror is the same person who was that cocky pre-teen in a picture with two friends, one was an old stand-by and the other, a pretty girl who wound up his prom date a couple of years later. This occurred, as a result of a fight with her boyfriend and somehow this cocky punk got to be the pinch hitter. This guy became the drugtaking forerunner of his group. The risk-taker, the person who believed he could leave after graduating college for the West Coast driving a car with a standard shift that he learned to master fifteen hundred miles into the trip. He made a living in the arts straight out of school then lost the belief that he could ever keep it up and instead dove under the covers of drug addiction. Driving a thousand miles one way with everything he owned then turned around and drove another thousand miles another way. Finally winding up back at his parents' house crying in his mother's arms as a complete failure, only to dwell in the depths of his addiction for the next five years. At twenty-nine, finally trying life clean. That was me. Given this miracle of hope. Dealing with years of professional failure but personal success growing ever so slowly. Starting a family and supporting them through limited means while never ceasing the search for creative sustainability. Going into my forties and finally receiving a few nods of approval. Almost too late to care but still able to cherish the successes. Fortifying each step of being in the creative life with some continuity. And reaching freedom from the day jobs by being led out of the workplace by men in uniforms. Humiliation that turned into exhilaration. Final acceptances that led to thinking of myself as a successful person who feels ok in his own skin. So many losses yet winding up feeling fine. Living like a king at the end though never having much money. Ideas turning into dreams somehow. Joy now bubbles through my being. Still can have bad days but mainly wake up excited. What else does one need? I can take care of myself after surviving adversity which took a lifetime to learn. I have endured many nightmares and awakened to a good life. Though it came late, it did come.

Chapter Three
OUTSIDE MYSELF

It was like being dropped into outer space. No more having to be somewhere. First, I thought I would keep working day jobs but soon learned no one wanted me. But after first feeling useless, I realized I was going to be truly free. It took a little while. I wanted to fight unfairness. I wanted to stand up for myself, too. By going for my freedom, I soon saw that I was going to do the right thing for myself. I had no one pressuring me to keep working. Didn't have to provide, commute, work in soul-killing environments as they are in social work. The draining of my energy always having dual careers. I was at the point where I didn't want to give to either track anymore. Audiences and actors did not deserve my effort for the time being, I believed. I had left it all on the field. I know that sounds strange and my therapist didn't get it either but I did. They just didn't deserve my passion, love, care, blood and sweat, the tears I always put into it. The long hours, the vulnerability, the financial drain. The entirety of producing and directing with no money to a continuity I constantly sought. The standard higher than what was available and just the sum of the pain it finally took to stop me. I went down for the count and came up wanting to create in a different way and all roads were now open. One day it entered my being… I can do what I want. What is it? And it began. I wrote about my life and the people in it. The false starts, the self-consciousness previously that colored my start. The fun, the pain, the different locales, all of it. It solved my unhappiness. It gave me solutions and changed my direction. I moved down South and the world stopped dragging me down with its mounting problems. The bad feelings, the toxins in the air and between people. A few wrong turns but mainly I was rejoicing in my new vocation. I stepped outside myself and granted myself what I felt I deserved. I started to see where I wasn't real. I got more real. My reality did not belong anymore where and with who I was with. I stepped outside myself and freely went my own way. I wound up in a hermit cabin not unlike the one I had created a piece about many years before. I now was there and remain there. And all went well for a while.

You see, one day I received a call that upset my equilibrium. It was from a woman from I knew years before. She had a request. She wanted me to respond to pictures she would send of herself. The thing about her was, she was not attractive but possessed great self-esteem. She both talked and behaved as if she was the most beautiful and desirable woman in the world. Always acted like that, I remembered.

She was also pretty crazy in general. She had been a very hard worker but was eternally complaining that she had to work. She felt she was entitled to be on Disability and hounded me to find a way for her to collect. This was the first thing I thought of when I heard from her. She had posted on the Internet a "worker of the month" award she had just won.

Anyway, the gist of her message was that she wanted to send these pictures of herself in various stages of undress and wanted reciprocity from me, old man that I am. It really was shocking! Also, though she was married, she had always carried on at the workplace as if she was endlessly man-crazy. I was totally alone on my mountain and it was Winter. I agreed to participate in this illicit adventure as a distraction from my hours of creativity. I was unclear where this would go. As I was hungry for contact, mostly absolutely alone and curious about this arrangement. I guess I forgot how mentally unbalanced she was. I was reminded of another time when this guy Johnny started stalking me this other time after we had a quarrel. Johnny, who always referred to himself in the third person was a workout nut and jogged all over town. He was in peak condition. After Johnny had been stalking me for months, I hung with this crazy gal Kitty, who one day said I know where Johnny lives and suggested we drive up to his place and stalk the stalker. Before I could answer her, she sped to Johnny's.

He was not there but he had a four-story garage in the middle of the woods, with a four-story mirror on the outside doors. He actually lived in a dilapidated shack next door. We high-tailed it out of there. Kitty was crazy but this caper provided me a perverse feeling to know these details about my stalker. Little while later, Johnny started up with this real nice guy who stood about six feet four and the guy cold cocked Johnny. Johnny stopped coming around after that. Anyway, this should have proven to me that I could play the fool for gals who are crazy. This adventure with Jillian, the one on the computer would take me on an out of body experience that I would take with me to the grave.

Chapter Four

JILLIAN AND THE WAR IN THE STREETS

ee Jillian wanted a clandestine relationship only on the computer in a protected setting. She wanted a debasing kind of exchange. Secretive was the main ingredient. That was to be the most important thing about it. I had nothing to lose but she did. She was married and I was not. She lived in a community which was also connected online. I was long gone. She wanted to display her wares but only in secret. The first installment came up. She was naked, overweight by a lot and shown only from behind in the shower. She turned her face around and said, "Join me", then spread and bent as far as she could and said, "split me, split me in two". She then demanded I get nude too and show my shrimped, little thing. Small by Time and medication's effect. She both laughed and cursed at me. Humiliated, I almost signed off but then she said she always wanted to be with me and Time's ravages didn't matter. That I still got her motor running and then abruptly went off the Internet. I stood stunned, creeped out and embarrassed all at once. I remained stunned for days. After a week, I heard from Jillian again. Here husband had beaten and abused her verbally. She had to wait for her opportunity to get back in touch. I almost said, "don't" but some kind of mixed bag of horror and compassion stopped me. I remained inert. I continued my level of isolation in my cabin abound Nature's wonder. Later that night, I saw she was posting about her finding a beauty supply line that changed her appearance and there were pictures of her that made her glamorous and unrecognizable. She asked the indulgence of her friends in both impossible and unrealistic ways to uphold their friendship of her and to be faithful to her troublesome life. She flirted outrageously with all she corresponded with and I just watched idly until she privately messaged, "in an hour, be on!"

An hour later, she appeared on my computer again naked, bent from behind and masturbated both her orifices and then put her fingers in her mouth. She then asked me to put my penis as close to the screen as possible and stay there. This went on repeatedly until two hours had passed. She then abruptly silently signed off.

I was getting disoriented on a daily basis alone in my solitude. I stopped being able to concentrate. I avoided the computer for days on end. I was upset by her connection with me and I was climbing the walls of my cabin with weirdness. I spent many hours wandering in the wilderness around my place but I couldn't think straight any longer. One day I was fishing by the cabin and I heard a sound near a lean to by the lake. All of a sudden there was a ding on my phone. It was Jillian in some new face change winking at me almost completely unrecognizable. I heard a bird screech, my heart pounding through my chest. "I'm too old for this", I said out loud. I could feel my Creator taking me out. I scurried home and took a nap. I dreamt of Jillian screaming my name over and over and her face which was not really her face erupting in orgasm. The face then froze and I woke up in a panic. "This has got to stop!" I muttered to myself. The following night I was summoned to the secret sexting that used to be a texting point. She was there again posing in the buff on top of her car in a garage. "Boris, you've got to come to me now." She said to me desperately. "I can't be without you, are you thinking of me?" Both shocked and unnerved, I agreed to anything she asked. "Jillian, I'll get on my way tomorrow". I said utterly helpless, surprising myself. "Give me a couple days to get up there". She whooped and jumped off the car and humped the hood before signing off.

On the way up to New York, I started thinking out of nowhere about this other woman we had worked with, Peggy Wood. She had no social boundaries and would always interrupt conversations that didn't involve her. She was gutless and upheld rules and spied on people for management. Nice overall but not too bright. She was the object of Jillian's scorn and her feelings of superiority over her. She couldn't hear too good and Jillian would play tricks on her all the time by spreading gossip but with words or names that Peggy would mistakenly confuse due to her hearing loss. Jillian would also soothe Peggy with massages in the office and Peggy would "ooh and ah" embarrassingly and carelessly inappropriate for the office. I kept thinking as I drove up if my prurient interest in Jillian's propositions had anything to do with her below the surface animosity toward Peggy and if I was to be used against her in some way. It had occurred to me that I really disliked both of these women immensely.

We met outside a trailer park where Peggy lived. Jillian wanted to surprise Peggy and didn't let her know of my presence. We first ate at a diner near the place of assignation. I watched as Jillian downed three burgers and multiple orders of fries with a couple of chocolate milkshakes. She told me that the excitement had triggered her massive appetite. I had very little to eat. I had driven many hours and wanted to stay still for a while and just rest. I found it difficult to just talk with Jillian and started thinking of meeting up with some friends in the area and catch up with them. But curious about this clandestine meeting kept me there until I almost passed out from fatigue. I excused myself and went to a motel and told Jillian I would see her and her friend in a couple of days. I checked in and made plans with the guys and regrouped. I wanted to find my bearings in my old community. I looked up some of the guys I hung with and they noticed how much I'd changed. Calmer and centered they said. How wrong they were! They asked me my plans and I said it was up to the fates. I left it at that. The next day I went to see Ann, my good friend. She had missed me terribly and we had kept up our correspondence over the years. She asked if I was ok. I sensed she saw through me but how could she? However, a true friend will sense something and I know she did. I let her know I had been lonely and thought of her many times. She said she felt the same but could never leave all her responsibilities in New York. I said I knew. She asked if I could stay awhile. I said I would think about it but I had to face some difficulties first. She dropped it. Another thing I did was go to my old haunts and think about the past and how I got to the place of paradise I had found. I thought also about the solitary confinement I had sentenced myself to. I had realized that people were ultimately hurtful to me and my experience taught me to live the life I had been living. I then watched television for hours as I had not done that for all the time I lived down South. Just with my writing, books and thoughts as I had designed it. My destiny had certainly been carved out. Yet Ann's request to think about returning kept revolving in my brain. If I had truly left my old life, why was I falling into this perverse abyss? Only my Creator knew.

In the distance, I heard a commotion. Things were happening in the streets. Conflict and noise. There were crowds massing. Troublemakers running the neighborhoods. Places that didn't have crime or stress were losing their immunity from these elements. The madness had been brewing and spreading while I had been away. All over the country, the streets were teeming. I wasn't prepared. I was so lost in my own little drama; I was oblivious to getting surrounded with what was swallowing our society. Groups of angry, crowding, meandering marauders were flying down the once quiet streets I had known. There was no respite from it. If you were older, you were a definite target. It began to really sink in. Sanity was scarce. Sobriety was lacking in the streets. Wisdom had flown the coop. It was a jungle rule. It was getting late. I could hear the noise. I was trying to meet the women again. I wanted to run back to Ann, but I couldn't. I had a date with destiny. All around I heard the roar now. I quickened my pace but my feet felt like cement blocks. Vision began to blur. Senses were getting dull. Oh, how I wish I was back home or at least with Ann. Sanctuaries for me. "Hey, get that old man!" I looked back. A whole bunch right behind me. I blacked out.

Chapter Five
A NEW NEST

---

*I*had been rescued by some good guys passing by. Evidently there had been a territorial war and the good guys won. I was safely brought to my friend Ann's house. She was my long-time and good friend. When I had been marched out of my last job like a criminal I went to Ann. She understood what had been going on. When I had been wrongly accused of robbing my aunt, she had helped me research the status of my aunt's Medicaid case which clearly showed the lie my family had put onto me. She had stood by me countless times. She allowed the guys to leave me all banged up and cared for me back to health. We never discussed what had brought me back up North. She didn't ask and I didn't go into it. She was on the battle lines of what was going on in the community. She had a high position in the social services business. She was a real good person and helped many people. After a while, I was getting uncomfortable in her place. Ann finally asked one day, "why are you here, Boris? I thought it was so magical where you were." I felt caught. I didn't want to lie to this special person. But the fires, loud voices and gunfire going off at night made me even more reticent to tell her the truth. "I just got restless, Ann, that's all." She sighed and left me alone.

But this signified a change in our coexistence. We started taking trips together when I was up to it. Getting out of town and spending time together on the road. It changed the atmosphere. She had plans to leave her job in the future. She wanted to know what I was going to do. "Let's just take it day by day", was all I could say. She sighed some more but we went on our trips and had a good time. Ithaca, Boston, New Hope, Pennsylvania. Lots of miles away from the contentious atmosphere in town. We could rely on each other.

Wasn't that enough? But she would start weeping out of nowhere. I felt unable to give her what she wanted. I wanted to but didn't. Once again in my life, I felt emotionally short. I started working on an opera. I had never written an opera before. I was once encouraged to try but it was a long time ago. Ann was very supportive. It got me through all the unease around us and inside of us. I was starting to get used to the life we were living. But a nagging tug went on inside me to get back to what I had come up to do. To see it through. Whatever that would be. With the other women. I looked at Ann searchingly. I started tearing up. I looked away. What was wrong with me? What? I made arrangements to pick up where I left off with Jillian and the assignation at the trailer park. I left Ann a note that I'd be in touch. That was it.

I went through the danger zone of the neighborhood. I got to Peggy's trailer park earlier than planned. I laid low and waited for Jillian. I prayed and called myself an old fool.

Before I go on, I need to say more about this opera I was getting lost in creating. In song, on one side was an overpowering chorus of Lust. On another side was this approaching roar of violence. This ominous presence enveloping an entire town. The music was drowning out goodness in favor of this approaching violence. The undercurrent was that lust was overcoming the beings and interrupting the sea of violence that awaited. At the same time, age was hampering my productivity. Fear and impotence were paralyzing me as the creator. Yes, it was all crashing within me. Parading through my obstacles on the street and facing the fear of the lustful meeting I had been pushing and pulling away from. It was all converging right there. Within me. I wished I was back at either Ann's place or back in my cabin but there I was pushing through the fear before I could get back to this life summation work. The opera. It reverberated through my mind as I had trudged along. Voices again rang out," get that old man" and had to stop in a backyard for a few harrowing moments as footsteps ran past. I turned and ran the other way. Breathing scarily heavily I reached the trailer park. Jillian soon came. She was very excited and pushed me into the empty trailer where Peggy awaited. Peggy recoiled from me as I imagined she would. The scar on her throat was very red and set off both my lust and anger equally. Again, I realized how much I didn't like either of them but really wasn't it me who I was railing against?

The action commenced with Jillian embracing me and then lining Peggy up for a backrub. I entered Jillian from behind as she removed Peggy's blouse and Peggy started moaning and soon turned around and they rubbed tits together. Peggy's were heavily nippled and Jillian's very round. They kissed again and again and soon Jillian ate Peggy. Her scar was turning redder and redder. She looked away from me until I turned her face into mine and violently kissed her. She melted. Jillian moved and put my prick deep into Peggy and Peggy shrieked and began to cry. Jillian began laughing maniacally. I came quickly, grabbed my clothes and ran out the back as I heard a door break down two men ran in and shot both women dead. I ran for a long time until I found my car and drove five hundred miles south. I fled that burning town and Ann. The end of my opera came into my head down the highway. All was done. Like a feverish doomsday dream.

Chapter Six
AT THE END OF MY HIGHWAY

I had been home for a while. For a few weeks, maybe a month I'd look out the window from time to time as if someone was coming for me. I had never written an opera and had to keep singing it into a recorder because I didn't know how to write or play music. I had however worked with music all my theatrical life. I sang it repeatedly so I would remember all of it. The words had become second nature after a while. Like a prayer that was running in front of me keeping me on the straight and narrow. Keeping me alive. Keeping me in survival mode. I was a man reaching the end of his road about to fork either to Hell or Salvation. Stuck between the road's direction in Act One. Act Two is the escape from the burning destruction around him. He gets a great insight that everyone is truly lost and we are all trying to outrun the burning of the sun. Salvation is the next morning's sun giving another gift of life.

Chapter Seven
OPERA IS BORIS', LIFE IS BEN'S

---

*H*is wondering if they would come after him is doused by the profound realization that everyone is outrunning their destruction. That there is no one left to come after an old man who only was somewhere he shouldn't have been.

Finally, he gets up the nerve to go out. A morning walk in the woods. Continuing on the road that goes into the little town he goes up the mountain that winds around the stream. That leads back to the road. Then goes through the woods. He has waved to the same people along the way he has encountered for years now. He is not on a schedule, no more hurry in his walk. He is out of discomfort and lucky again to be home. His environment that he chose. The town, the land and his house. The opera went out to his agent. Done on his end and probably never another. Maybe sleep for a long, long time. He thought of maybe a leisurely trip somewhere. Maybe a long rest from all that effort during the nonsense. He had no more business with anything. He saw in his mail there was a letter from Ann. He would read it later. He remained somewhat unresolved in the matter of Ann. He thought of the peace he had before the encounter with the women. He thought of the desire for peace he had before he came down South. He thought of the sanctuary Ann had provided during his stressful time up North and how she didn't push to know anything he didn't want to reveal.

He went into a dream. The opera remained now in his dream. In dream form. The long highway that had been his life was running out of road. The people who had been in his life had all but disappeared. If the one person in his life who cared, he might not have enough miles left to offer. She was on the cusp of her own self -discovery. Her own destiny of choice which had been put on the shelf for many years. He felt he had no right to contribute to her own decision. She had to find it herself. She might already dwell in it for all he knew. The opera was drawing to a close. The echo of the curtain's finale was anticipated with great excitement. Anticipation always drove Ben Levis to his actions. Yes, we are now discussing Ben Levis again.

Ben went to get the letter from Ann with the anticipation of a young man. He still had his hopes. As always, there was high mindedness and there was the fact that Ben was a human being, after all.

www.ingramcontent.com/pod-product-compliance
Lightning Source LLC
Chambersburg PA
CBHW021448240626
47154CB00005B/1761